# IN LOVE WITH A DOWN SOUTH HOODLUM 2

MZ. BIGGS

Cole Hart

**In Love With A Down South Hoodlum 2**



Published in the United States of America.



Published by Cole Hart Signature, LLC.

**Mailing List**

**To stay up to date on new releases, plus get information on contests, sneak peeks, and more,**

***Go To The Website Below...***

**www.colehartsignature.com**

## CHECK OUT THESE OTHER GREAT BOOKS BY MZ. BIGGS:

See What Had Happened Was: A Contemporary Love Story (Part: 1-3)

Yearning For The Taste of A Bad Boy (Part: 1-3)

Dirty South: A Dope Boy Love Story (Part: 1)

Falling for A Dope Boy (Part: 1-3)

Feenin' For That Thug Lovin' (Part: 1-3)

A Bossed Up Valentine's (Anthology)

Jaxson and Giah: An Undeniable Love (Part: 1-2)

Finding My Rib: A Complicated Love Story (Part: 1)

In love With My Cuddy Buddy (Part: 1-2/Collaboration)

Your Husband's Cheating On Us (Part: 1-3)

From Cuddy Buddy To Wifey: Levi and Raven's Story (Standalone/Collaboration)

In Love With My Father's Boyfriend (Standalone)

Your Husband's Calling Me Wifey (Standalone)

She's Not Just A Snack... She's A Whole Buffet: BBWs Do It Better (Standalone)

Blood Over Loyalty: A Brother's Betrayal (Standalone)

Married to the Community D (Part: 1-2)

Downgraded: From Wifey to Mistress (Part: 1-3)

A Mother's Prayer (Part: 1-2)

Heart of A Champion... Mind Of A Killer (Standalone)

Turned Out By My Husband's Best Man (Standalone)

Ain't No Lovin' Like Gulf Coast Lovin' On The $4^{th}$ of July (Novella)

This Is Why I Love You (A Novella)

The Hood Was My Claim To Fame (A Novella)

A Killer Valentine's (Anthology)

Bouncing Back After Zaddy Gave Me The Clap (Standalone)

Tantalizing Temptations in New Orleans (An Erotic Novella)

Santa Blessed Me With a Jacktown Boss (Novella)

Diamonds and Pearls (Standalone)

Dating A Female Goon (Standalone/Collaboration)

Pregnant By My Best Friend's Husband (Part: 1-2)

Wifed Up By A Down South Boss (Thug Love Collection)

Creepin' With The Plug Next Door (Part: 1-3)

Creepin' With My Co-Worker (Part 1)

Crushin' On A Dope Boy: Cashae and Tay (Box Set)

The Autobiography of A Boss's Wife (Collaboration)

Scorned By The Love Of A Thug

The Thug Is Mine (Part:1/Collaboration)

Every Dope Boy Got A Side Chick: Kenyon & Milani's Story (Box Set)

A Boss And A Hood Chick (Part: 1-3)

Yo' So Called Bae Creepin With Me (Part: 1-2)

In Love With A Down South Hoodlum (Part: 1)

# AUTHOR'S NOTE:

Please take the time to leave an honest review on either Amazon or Goodreads after reading the book. Again, your support is greatly appreciated. Also, feel free to reach out to me anytime via the contact information listed below. Happy Reading...

-Mz. Biggs

# WANT TO CONNECT WITH ME? HERE'S HOW:

Email: authoress.mz.biggs@gmail.com
Twitter: @mz_biggs
TikTok: @mz.biggs
Instagram: mz.biggs
Goodreads: Mz. Biggs
Facebook: Authoress Mz. Biggs
Look for my Reading Group on Facebook:
Lounging with Mz. Biggs

# WHERE WE LEFT OFF:
## EVELYN (LYN)

"Can I ride home with y'all?" I waltzed back inside the restaurant and asked my parents when Corde' drove away. He left me standing there with no real explanation of what was going on. That bothered me. It put me back in the mindset of the way that Logic used to do things. I didn't want a repeat relationship of that. Why should I be kept in the dark about things when I was his partner? I needed to know everything that was going on so I wouldn't receive any surprises.

"Why? Where's Corde'?" my father questioned. He stood from his seat and walked over to me. He took my hand and guided me out of the restaurant. It was no secret to him the line of work that Corde' was in so it was no question why he took me outside. He wanted to get me out of earshot of others. "What's going on, Lyn?"

"I dunno. We were walking outside, and he got some text. He asked me to go home with you and mom and said that he would explain everything later."

"What's his number?" my father asked.

"Why?" I returned.

"So, I can figure out what's going on. Has he ever done anything like this before?'

"No, and I don't like it. It's really starting to get to me. I don't want him to be the same way Logic was," I explained.

"Trust me... If he were anything like Logic, you would've run by now. You loved Logic true enough. However, there were a lot of things in your relationship that you weren't happy about. You think because you talked to your mother about it and not me, that she wouldn't tell me? I know everything." I could've died when he said that. It had me wondering what all my mother said to him that I didn't know about. "Don't worry, Lyn. You are in a no judgement zone from me and your mother, you know that" he told me. That did make me feel a little better. Although, I couldn't get Corde' off my mind. I wanted to call him, but I couldn't. I didn't want him to think I wasn't respecting his need for privacy.

"Can you take me somewhere?" I asked him.

"Take you where?" he probed.

"Either you can take me or not. I will tell you everything you need to know on the way. I need some answers," I expressed.

"Say no more. I already know where we're headed," he advised me. He left me standing outside while he went back inside to get my mother. She came running outside as if the building were on fire. I threw my hand up to stop her from saying anything. The last thing I wanted to do was talk to anybody about anything. I needed to clear my head, and this was going to be the only way to do it.

My father got his car and pulled it to the front of the restaurant. My mother and I hopped inside. Her in the front and me in the back. The whole time we rode, my father had gospel music playing. He must've had the same feeling I had. Something was wrong. Whatever it was, I wanted to get to the bottom of it. I couldn't take being in limbo and not knowing what was going on. The information Benedict had given me was too much. There had to be some confusion in what he said because it didn't add up.

By the time we had arrived at the house I once shared with

Logic, my stomach began to quiver. My mind was all over the place. I'd gotten people to come in and fix the house up, but I never actually sold it the way I was supposed to. It was my way of hanging on. Mentally, I let go of things in the church that day, but my heart was still holding on. Corde' told me not to try to be with him until I was ready, yet I still wanted him. I started to feel like I'd moved too fast and all of this with him may have been a mistake.

"What are we doing here?" my mother asked while I was getting out of the car.

"She needs some type of closure. She's the only person that can give it to herself and if being here is what she needs to get it then we are going to sit here until she does. You are more than welcomed to Uber home."

"Uber home? The hell I look like to you? I'm not Ubering shit. I didn't Uber here, did I?"

"I'm saying, if you're going to complain then you need to find a way home. She needs us right now and I'm not moving until she's ready."

"Then you sit here with her and y'all can Uber home. This place gives me the creeps."

They sat in the car and continued to argue. I wasn't worried about them leaving me. My father would never do that. Truth be told, my mother wouldn't either. She was being a hard ass just because.

Taking my time, I used my key to unlock the door. When I entered, all types of feelings hit me. I closed my eyes and visualized Logic coming to the door and greeting me. If I could have those days back, I'd gladly accept them. He did me wrong, but he was a good man. I'd never wish death on anyone. Continuing throughout the house, I went straight back to the dreaded closet. The one where my life had changed significantly.

Standing outside the doorway, I allowed tears to drop from my eyes. The events of that night began to play out in my head. It was sickening the way they came in and destroyed my life. The way they murdered him like he was some animal. His life was worth more than anything they were probably searching for. That reminded me of the safe. I'd cleared it out except for a box that he had kept in there. He had a key to it, but I never knew where he kept it. After what Benedict said, I had to find a way to get inside the box. Logic had hidden something from me, and I was sure that the box contained everything that I needed to know.

It took me a while to gather myself before I could go inside the closet. When I did, it seemed as though my heart was going to beat out of my chest. The amount of anxiety I was experiencing felt unreal. Suddenly, I heard footsteps coming up the stairs. I blocked out my anxiety and rushed over to the safe. It was open and the box was gone. It didn't take me long to figure out what happened.

***Knock... Knock...***

The distinct knock on the door was what I needed to confirm what I already knew.

"Hello Logic. It's nice to see you finally came out of hiding," I greeted him.

Logic came up behind me and hugged me from the back. He never said a word. I couldn't deny that it felt good to be in his arms again. I didn't know why. He'd not only lied to me, but he'd faked his death. But why? When Benedict told me that he was still alive, I just knew he was lying. However, I knew that if nothing else, Logic loved this house. He wouldn't have to go anywhere since he had a whole funeral and left people to believe that he was dead. Who would come searching for him at that point? I knew his damn body didn't flop right when I kicked his ass out of the casket. He should've been moving around like a fish out of water. Instead, all I heard was a loud thud.

"Why?" I queried. He needed to tell me what was going on that was so bad that he had to pretend as if he were dead. That shit hurt a lot of people, including me. People had to change their lives because of it. Me. His so-called real wife. Kosine. The members of his crew. It was ridiculous. Logic had been selfish, and I wanted him to tell me why.

As I was turning around to look into his eyes, my vision became dark. He'd put something over my head. No matter how I fought him to remove it, I was unable to. He was too strong for me.

"Stop fighting it. It's time for you to come home where you belong, baby girl," were the last words I heard before I was knocked out.

***(To Be Continued...)***

# I
# LOGIC

It's only right that I have the chance to properly introduce myself. Logic was the name that my parents gave me. Why? The hell if I knew. It fit me perfectly. There was not shit that I did that didn't have logic or a reason (for the folks in the back) for it to be done.

Some shit had hit the fan and I had to get the hell out of dodge. My supposed murder was staged and Kosine was in on it the entire time. Who staged it? Me, of course. So, who was crazy enough to try to kill me? Day-Day's punk ass! Then he had the nerve to go after my bitch when he was the one responsible for trying to take me out.

Day-Day was a heavy hitter in the streets. A real down south hoodlum. That nigga caused problems wherever he went. Shit, as long as he'd been in the game, he'd never been seen with a bitch. So why now? Why my bitch? When Kosine told me what was going on, I had to come out of hiding. Sure, there was a lot of shit that I kept from Lyn, but again, there was a reason behind it.

The only reason I went into hiding was because Kosine told me that there was too much heat on me. I wasn't sure how he knew, but I trusted him. He didn't have a reason to lie to me.

Not one I could think of. I needed time to find out what was going on. Faking my death was the only way for me to do it. Kosine said he knew when Day-Day was sending someone after me. He claimed he heard it from some cat on the street. That night, I had the little gathering at my crib so everyone could be there. When it was over, I had a few niggas camping out in different places. That way, I'd have backup when shit went down. Kosine agitating Lyn was part of the plan. I knew she'd storm off and head to the room. That was the only way I could get her out of the way so that we could do what we needed to do in order to set up for the "hit". Things went exactly the way that Kosine said they were going to go. Hell, I was thankful somebody told him what was up because they were there to get me out of the house right on time.

The one part that was not a part of the plan was my attempt to kill Lyn. I had learned about her sleeping with Kosine a few days earlier and kept trying to find a way to handle the shit. When we put the plan together, I figured something might go wrong. If I were to die, there was no way I was leaving Lyn alive to be with another nigga. However, them niggas came in before I could carry out what I set out to do. Kill her. The more I thought about it, the more I was able to see that it was a good thing that they came in when they did. What I was thinking was correct. Lyn's ass was quick to move on to the next nigga. She couldn't be trusted. She needed to die. At least now, she'd be able to die with the mufucka she betrayed me for.

Kidnapping her was not the ideal way to get to her, but knowing the type of woman she was, I knew she wouldn't go with me willingly when she saw me. Knocking her out was the only choice I had. It was easy to get her out the back of the house because her crazy ass parents were standing in the driveway fussing over something dumb. I was positive of that, it was a habit for them.

We spent the night on the road driving to Atlanta. Why there? It was where we knew Day-Day was headed. He tried to set me up, so we returned the favor. His sister was the only family he had. We found that out doing research of our own.

"Are you sure you want to do this?" Kosine asked me, removing me from my thoughts.

"Why would I not? The minute he came after me, he started a war. He should've known that shit. He thinks he's the man in these streets and he's not. It's me. You hear that? IT'S ME, NIGGA!" I raised my voice finding myself annoyed with the entire situation all over again.

"Hell, it's me too! Fuck wrong with you?" Kosine spoke. For some reason, he always found the need to speak about his status in my life. It was not needed and definitely not important. He thought he was bigger than he was, and he wasn't. Trying to tell him that was out of the question. He would get in his feelings like he was doing now and would be ready to argue all night. Sometimes he acted just like a bitch. I wasn't sure how I dealt with him for as long as I did. If he wasn't my cousin, I would've cancelled his ass a long time ago. It didn't help that he was making dumb ass moves in the streets and doing shit without thinking or talking to me about it first. That only gave me extra shit to deal with and I didn't have time for that.

"You heard what I said?" he asked.

I almost said, "Yeah, I heard you, bitch," since that was how he was acting. However, I chose to carefully address his big black wannabe baby ass.

"Yeah, I heard you. You don't count. You're my right-hand. You'll always be second in command." Kosine's nose started twitching. He was either pissed or that coke had him faded. Either way, he knew not to say the wrong damn thing to me. He had to be careful with his words too. He was quick to fight niggas. I was quick to shoot niggas. It was best to pick your battles with me as well and he knew that.

"Yeah. Whatever. I'm as important as you, nigga. Don't you fuckin' forget it. If it weren't for me, you would really be sleeping with the worms. The fuck!" he angrily spat.

"Ko, this is my only time telling you this. You're my cousin and right-hand man. I'm loyal to you and I expect the same in return. What I won't do is allow you to talk to me any kind of way. We both know who the fuck is in charge. I won't tolerate your disrespect. If you come out the side of your neck with me, I'ma come out the side of my neck with you and shit on your day. I don't give a fuck who you are. Either talk to me with respect or don't talk to me at all. We not gonna sit here and act like we don't know who's in charge. You are my second in command. If something were to happen to me, that's when you're supposed to step the fuck up and handle things. Think about how that shit turned out and you were only on a trial run while I was hiding. You aren't ready to be in charge. You know it. I know it. Hell, the world knows it. You think with your emotions and not with your head. That shit is going to land you in jail or in the grave. It's your choice," I sternly spoke.

Luckily for him we'd reached our destination. Dealing with Lyn was going to be a task in itself, so I was not about to sit there and argue with him. Ko could either shit or get off the toilet at this point. I was back in control and there wasn't shit him or anyone else could do about it. Throwing the car in park, I hopped out.

"Get her out," I instructed him and kept walking inside the house to be met with a nagging ass Nayonni.

"Untie me right now. I'm going to kill you," she hollered. That was Day-Day's sister. She was fine as hell. If she learned how to behave, she could have the chance to be my third wife. I laughed to myself at the thought of it.

Kosine came inside the house. He walked past me without saying a word. I had to be tripping. I knew I told him to get Lyn out the car, but he walked in the house empty handed.

"Where is she?" I asked him.

"In the car where you left her. I'm not your damn 'do boy'. You want something done, get one of those lame ass bottom of the barrel workers to do it or do the shit yourself. You gon' respect me too, mufucka!" he spat.

"You big mad or naw?" I chuckled. I wasn't about to argue with him. He was in his feelings for whatever reason. That meant he was someone I was going to have to keep an eye on. He was acting suspect as hell. He said he was my brother, but he was acting like my enemy. At this point, I couldn't trust anybody.

Apparently, Lyn needed to be added to the list of people I couldn't trust. It hadn't been a good three months since I was supposedly executed, and she had already gotten under the next man. Where was the loyalty? She was supposed to love me for the rest of her life. Moving on was not an option. Not this damn soon. It was good that we had that long ass drive ahead of us because it gave me time to think 'bout the most appropriate way for me to approach the situation with her. I didn't want to be too brash and make her scared of me. However, she needed to know that there was going to be a price to pay for her not being loyal.

Since Kosine wanted to be an ass, I shot a text to one of the workers to let them know to bring Lyn inside. She was still knocked out, so I had them take her to the bedroom I had set up for her.

"Who the fuck is that?" Nayonni inquired.

"Mind your fuckin' business. This ain't got shit to do with you," I fumed.

"It does when you have me somewhere I don't want to be. Why the hell am I here? What do you want from me?" she asked.

"Shut up!" I yelled. I was sick of hearing her voice. She knew exactly why she was here. Playing stupid was not good for her.

Nayonni thought she was fooling me. She must've figured that since we'd never met before, I had no knowledge of who she was. She was dead ass wrong. She was just as deadly as her brother. Hell, from what I heard, she was worse than him and that's why she lived a carefree life. She thought nobody would touch her ass. In the past, that may have been the case, but it wasn't anymore. When they came for me, they fucked up.

"You know what. Since you want to talk so much, tell me who sent you after me. Who was crazy enough to pay you and your brother to try to take me out?" I snarled. She started laughing. Wasn't shit funny. It was pissing me off even more.

"My brother? Who is my brother?" She stared into my eyes with her big beautiful brown eyes.

Nayonni had my dick jumping in my pants from how fine she was. She was a big bitch though. Not big as in fat and even if she was, that wouldn't have mattered. I preferred a BBW over a skinny bitch any day of the week. I wanted my woman to be the same as the way I lived my life, dangerous and with plenty of curves. But back to Nayonni, she had to be damn near six feet tall. She was thick in all the right places, with a milk chocolate skin tone, high cheek bones, wide hips, a fat ass, plump breasts, and big ass lips. I was ready to do something to her. She had the type of ass I could lay on and do planks. That mufucka was huge. I loved that shit. She had a beautiful smile and flawless skin. That added to her sexiness to me.

From doing surveillance on her, I noticed that she always kept herself up. She always dressed nice and her hair was always done in a different style. The one thing I didn't care for was the amount of weave that she wore. I preferred for my woman to be more on the natural side. I'd never gotten the chance to see her real hair because of all the weave. Shit, if she was baldheaded, she needed to embrace it. Hell, baldheaded hoes needed love too. Plus, I felt like I could help her with that. *I'd fuck her so good, hair would sprout out of her scalp like limbs on a tree*, I thought to myself. One thing I could say was that I was at least glad that her body was real and not paid for. She had these big, bright, brown eyes that were mesmerizing. Yeah, I wanted her on my team. With her and Lyn, I'd be walking around with two of the baddest bitches to ever grace this earth.

"Uh, hellooooo... Are you deaf now? Who is this so-called

brother? My mother only pushed one child out of her pussy and that was me."

"Don't play with me, Nayonni. I know that Day-Day is your brother. You may be your mother's only child, but your pops had a weak ass pull out game. That nigga left a baby wherever he went."

"Who the hell is Day-Day? I don't know no damn Day-Day. I don't even have a damn

bro-"

***Smack...***

Before she could finish speaking, I backhanded her. She was lying to me. If there was one thing I couldn't stand it was a mufuckin' liar. She was supposed to be some big bad bitch in the streets. She could've at least held true to her title. Why bitch up and not speak facts? Was staying alive that important that she had to lie?

"Hit me again," she instructed. Blood was running down the side of her mouth. I observed her as she began giggling like a schoolgirl before moving her tongue around in her mouth and spitting blood damn near across the room.

"Go ahead and hit me. You only did that shit because I'm tied to this damn chair. Untie me and try it again," she urged me. "I'm not that same bitch Kosine has upstairs. You know, the one that's his fuckin' punching bag. I'll knock your dick through your back," she added.

"Good one. You really think you can beat me? You really have shit twisted, ma. You better be glad I don't hit bitches. If I did, you'd been sitting in this bitch seeing stars floating around your head and shit."

"Nigga, please. You hit women. You just know which women to hit. Besides, didn't your fuckin' ass smack me not to long ago? I'm a full-blown woman so that clearly means that you hit women. Go ahead and try me again," she taunted me.

She was clearly trying to get under my skin, and I wasn't about to let that happen. If she wanted to play with someone, she needed to go play with her baldheaded mammy because I was not the one to be played with.

"Goodnight," I told her. I leaned in to place a kiss on her right cheek, winked at her, and left her ass sitting in the same chair she'd been in since we picked her ass up.

Day-Day thought he was on his way to see his sister by the text that was sent, when he was really on his way to pay Kosine and I a visit. Coming after me was the worst decision he could've ever made in his life and he was about to find that out the hard way.

# 2

## NAYONNI (YO-YO)

Nayonni was my birth name but everyone called me Yo-Yo. Corde', better known in the streets as Day-Day, was indeed my brother. That's why I had to protect him at all cost. We pretty much were one in the same when it came down to this street shit. We'd been hitting the streets heavy since we were younger.

Day-Day and I grew up in the foster care system. Our mother was a single mother, and it was hard for her. She met a man who told her he loved her but that he couldn't be with her because he wasn't ready for kids and the only kids he would ever want to deal with were kids that came from his shriveled-up balls. Since being with him was the most happiness she'd ever received in life, she was quick to give us up. She placed us on the steps of the local fire department and didn't look back. That was all she wrote. I was five at the time and Day-Day was three. We were young but that was some shit I'd never forget. How could I when all the foster homes we went to weren't worth a damn?

When I was thirteen, I met an older man, Johnny Boy. Since I'd always been built like a grown woman, it was easy for me to convince him that I was eighteen. He never asked for an ID. Then I made sure to dress how a grown woman did. When I explained to him that I had a younger brother and we were about to be out on the streets, he had no problem finding a place for us to go. He was an assassin. He had money. He put me up in a condo and made sure my brother and I had everything we needed.

One day, I asked him if he'd let me go out with him to see what he did. He obliged. The first kill I saw him do was hard as hell. I had nightmares. Then he showed me the money he made behind that kill. That was when I let that nightmare shit go. I put my heart on ice and asked if I could work for him. He told me I could work with him and not for him. That made me fall in love with him. Any man that allowed me to walk beside him and not put me behind him was a winner for me. Things started to look up in my life. As I continued to get older and get better at this killing shit, Day-Day asked about joining in. I didn't have a problem with it. Shit, we'd had it hard coming up. If there was a way to avoid living that hard ass life again, I was all for it. I took him under my wing the way my old man had done me, and he was a pro in no time.

Johnny Boy ended up being killed when I was sixteen. He had money stashed away that only he and I knew about so that helped a lot. Any jobs he had out there were shifted over to me since the people he worked for were fully aware that we worked together. With Johnny Boy gone, Day-Day and I became partners. That was the best decision I could've ever made. We were close but us working together brought us closer. We'd had each other's back then and we got each other's backs now.

One thing I could say was that no matter what we were doing in these streets, we always made sure we had our asses in class, every day. Getting caught in the streets was not an option. They would find out we had run away from foster care and put us back in the system. The only reason they didn't know that we had already run away was because I made sure to break my foster parents off each month. Plus, they were still getting money from the state. As long as we showed our face on the day the social worker came, we were able to get away with the shit.

Johnny Boy's death was hard on me. I went into a deep depression and I couldn't eat, drink, shit, or sleep. A lot of the jobs I was assigned to do Day-Day had to do for me. It didn't help that I was pregnant. I hid the pregnancy up until it was time for me to have him. I gave him up for adoption because of the life I lived. I moved around too much and was nowhere near a nurturer. So, I had to do what was best for my child. Please know that I picked the family and I maintained contact with them. I knew where my child was and spoke with him frequently. He knew who I was and didn't seem to harbor any bad feelings toward me. It had always been in my mind to tell him, when he was old enough, why I did what I did. His adoptive parents knew the plan and agreed to it. Besides, they also knew that crossing me was not going to end well for them.

"You find, ma. What's yo name?" A short guy that I'd never seen before entered the room. He reminded me of Lil' Duval, only he was darker, and his face was fatter. Come to think of it, his whole damn body was fatter. He had to have been slow because that was the way he talked. The fact that he was hitting on me almost made me vomit in my mouth.

"Find? Do you mean fine?" He didn't even know how to use proper English. I wanted him out of my presence immediately.

"That's I said," he grunted.

"You mean that's what you said? And no, that was not what you said. You good? You need help with grammar and English, I see."

"Bitch, fuck you," he muttered and came rushing toward me as if he were about to hit me. I closed my eyes and prayed that he would. His ass was going to be another nigga added to my "Kill List".

"Damn, is it a requirement that all y'all have fucked up attitudes to work for Logic?" I probed. There wasn't a single man that came through there that had a good attitude. He must not have been paying them enough to put up with his egotistical ass. "Why do you work for him when you are clearly unhappy?" I needed an ally, so I had to try my best to get on his good side. Why not be nice, right? It didn't hurt to try. If it didn't work, I'd try something else.

"Who said I was unhappy?"

"The fact that you hollered at me when I was simply helping you tells me that you're unhappy."

"Stop trying to diagnose me or play those mine games you're known for playing. I know all about you," he chided.

"First of all, it's mind games and I don't have to play them with someone who doesn't have a damn mind. You can't even use correct English and that's annoying as fuck. If you're able to pull women, they have to be retarded as hell. Ain't no way in hell you'd lay your big ass on top of me giving me shitty sex talk. You'd be better off singing *Old McDonald Had A Farm*. That seems to be more along the lines of the English you can speak. Second of all, you think you know about me. I can assure you that you know absolutely nothing about me. Why don't you ask me anything you want to know?"

I gave him the floor. He had to be pissed by the way that I spoke to him. Yet, I could see that it also made him feel good. I could tell by the twinkle in his eye. That was dumb to me. Just because I told him to ask me what he wanted to know didn't mean I was going to answer him or be truthful in my answer.

"Why did you come after Logic? He doesn't fuck with nobody."

Already, he'd made me mad. He must've been drunk or high or something. He had forgotten that quick the type of work they did. Logic was always doing shit to people. He was a big ass bully. People could say what they wanted, but he was no better than Kosine in my opinion.

"You do know who you work for, right? Or did you forget? Logic may be a good man to the people on his team, but he is a piece of shit to people he doesn't know and don't give a damn about. What man that's such a good person would have a woman tied to a chair without food or water? Then I have to get escorts to go to the fuckin' bathroom. What kind of shit is that?"

"That's your fault. Had you not tried to kill him then you wouldn't be in the situation you are in."

"I don't know what the hell you are talking about, but I did not try to kill that nigga. He ain't ever did shit to me so why would I try to kill him?" The shit wasn't adding up. Somebody had to have set me up and I was going to find out who the hell it was.

Logic kept asking about my brother and now this clown saying we tried to kill Logic. Where the hell were they getting their information from? Day-Day and I hadn't even been doing jobs like that for a while. We decided we'd gotten more than enough money to get out of the business of assassinating people. Shit, we had one last job to do and that was it. That job had nothing to do with Logic or any of his people. So, it was really crazy how they kept saying that we were the ones responsible for going after him. I had to figure out who the shit came from.

"Where did you get that shit from? I would never go after Logic and if I did, he would've really been dead. Check my record. When I aim, I don't miss," I assured him. Those were facts. Nobody that I have ever been hired to kill has been able to walk away or hide. That was because they never saw me coming. That was the same for Day-Day. Somebody was setting us up, but why?

"Kosine did his research. He told us that someone sent you and Day-Day to kill Logic. We were ten steps ahead of y'all in our plan, so you weren't able to get to him. Now you over there looking stupid because you tied up and won't be making it out of this shit alive."

"Kosine? That's the most unloyal ass nigga in the game. Why the hell would he listen to him?"

"That's his family. Kosine ain't got no reason to lie to any of us."

"Yeah, aight. That's when you really need to check your facts. Family will sometimes lie to you before the next person. Especially people like Kosine. That nigga's pores drips jealousy. That's who the hell you need to be looking at. I can assure you that I did not try to kill Logic. That nigga would be dead DEAD!"

"What about your brother?"

"What brother? I keep telling y'all that I don't have a brother. Stop trying to give me one. Damn. Y'all dumb," I sassed. It was not my job to confirm to them that I had a brother. If anything, I needed to make them believe that they had the wrong chick, but I'd already said too much so it was a little too late for that. However, another thought came to my mind. When I pissed dude off earlier, he was about to come after me. If I could actually get him to do it then there was an opportunity for me to get away.

"You are going to stop playing with us, Yo-Yo. We aren't dumb. We know who you are and what you're about. You won't get away with this."

"Your fat ass doesn't know shit. You think you know. You should've done a little more research about me. Don't worry, I'm going to get out of this and when I do, I'm coming for your whole family. I'ma torture them and make you watch. Then, I'm going to feed them to you. You shouldn't have a problem eating them since it doesn't look like you've ever missed a meal in life," I taunted.

"Bitch, fuck you," he spat.

"Fuck me? You wish you could. You probably can't even find your dick. That mufucka probably so small, it's curled up like a pig's tail." I began laughing loudly. He was dark but that nigga was turning bright red. I had done a good job getting him mad. His ass took off running toward me. As soon as he did, he knocked the chair over and I went flying to the ground.

They were dumb. The chair I was in was already wobbly. When they would leave me in the room alone, I would wiggle in it more to get it weaker. I knew that one big fall would make it come apart and I'd be able to break free, and that's exactly what happened. As soon as the chair hit the floor, it broke into pieces and I was able to free myself from the ropes they had me tied with. Apparently, he hit his head during the fall because he was out cold. Now, all I had to do was get that fat mufucka off me.

It was a struggle, but I was finally able to push him off of me. Thank God I stayed in the gym. With him out of the way, I had to pace myself yet be quick on my feet. There was no way I'd be able to get out of the house tonight, so I was going to have to find a good place to hide. However, I had to make them think that I was on the run. Kosine and Logic had men outside the house, but no one was inside. Idiot ass moves on their part. It gave me the chance to look around to see what I could find. There had to be some place I could hide that they wouldn't think to look for me. The house was fully furnished so it shouldn't be that hard, right? Wrong!

A buzzing sound caught me off guard. I thought someone was coming so I jumped behind the couch trying to take cover. Not before grabbing the lamp off the table. If I had to fight my way out, I was going to do my best to do so. After sitting there for a while and nobody appeared, I thought maybe I was hearing things. That was until the buzzing sound started again. It hit me that his phone was ringing. I needed to get to it so I could reach out to my brother. He was the only one that would be able to get me out of this mess. Calling the police was out of the question. When Day-Day and I came back to retaliate, we didn't need any interference.

Staying low, I crawled over to the man. Urgently, I searched his body for his phone. It was in his back pocket. Holding it in front of his face, I allowed his face ID to unlock it. Not wanting to risk it locking back before I had a chance to use it, I went to his settings and took the lock off the phone. I slid the phone into my pocket and went back to trying to find a place to hide. I opened the window in the living room to give them the illusion that I had snuck out and then headed for the attic. I made sure I was as quiet as possible since it was upstairs. The least little sound that I made would give me away and I couldn't allow that to happen.

Strategically, I took each step one at a time. I placed my feet along the outer parts to avoid the squeaking that normally happened when you stepped in the middle. It felt like it took me forever to get to the top of the stairs. I searched around as best I could with no light to see where the attic was. It was hard as hell. I couldn't use the flashlight on the phone because I would be at risk of someone seeing it. I couldn't afford that. This was a time that being somewhat tall gave me an advantage. I stuck both of my arms in the air and walked from one end of the hall to the other, slow as hell, until I felt the string for the attic door.

"That's right, Merc. Suck daddy dick," I heard Kosine say out of nowhere. My skin crawled. I couldn't believe Mercury was suckin' that nigga's crusty dick after the way he'd drug her through the damn house the day before. I guess she was doing what she had to do. Couldn't have been me. His ass would've been somewhere tied to an anchor at the bottom of the fuckin' ocean. Kosine would have me so fucked up. The same way he and Logic had me fucked up now. I was waiting for the perfect opportunity, and I was going to get both of their asses.

"It's been an hour; can I stop now?" Hearing Mercury say that almost brought a tear to my eye. She was trying to stick up for herself. That was a start. "Please, can I stop?" I heard her ask again, removing me from my thoughts.

***Smack...***

"You'll stop when I tell you to stop. Now suck my dick the way I like it before I fuck you up," Kosine hollered at her after hitting her. It almost made me want to bust through the door and help her but fuck all that. When they left the house, the only people there were Mercury and me. She could've tried to help a sister out, but she didn't. For that very reason, she was on her own.

Minding the business that paid me, I took my time to pull

the door to the attic down. It made a screeching noise when I almost had it all the way down. I rushed up the steps and closed it back behind me. Once inside the attic, I moved over to a corner and threw an old, dusty blanket over my head to keep myself camouflaged. I prayed hard as hell that nobody would come checking to see where that noise came from.

After roughly ten minutes had passed, I felt safe. Removing the phone from my back pocket, I was about to send Day-Day a text until I realized that I didn't know his number. I'd gotten so complacent with the phone storing numbers for me that I never took the time to learn his number. I was pissed at myself. Nothing was working the way that I needed. It was then that I made up in my mind that I was getting out of there come hell or high water.

# 3

# EVELYN (LYN)

*THE NEXT DAY*

Waking up the next morning, I was confused by where I was. I attempted to stand to walk around and see what was going on. I needed some idea of where I could've been. As I got out the bed, I realized I couldn't get far. A sharp pain hit me in my abdomen and between my legs. That caused me to sit back down on the edge of the bed. Not to mention, one of my hands had been tied to the bed so I couldn't really move. When I woke up the night before, Logic was sweet to me and I wasn't tied to anything. It made me wonder what changed throughout the night to make him go out of his way to keep me here.

"HELLLLLPPPPP!" I yelled. Logic had done this, and he was very strategic. There was no way anybody would be able to hear me, but I had to try anyway.

"Why are you hollering, baby girl? You know I would never do anything to hurt you," I heard his voice.

"Why are you doing this?"

"Doing what? Bringing my wife to our new home?"

"I'm not your wife. You're married to Kazya."

"Okay, so our marriage license is a fake, but what does that matter? Didn't I come home to you every night? Didn't I make sure you were always taken care of?" He came over to me and ran the back of his hand down the side of my face. I jumped off the bed and back from him. He didn't need to touch me. I didn't want him anywhere near me.

"Why are you moving away from me, Lyn? You're pissing me off."

"You think I care about you being pissed off? Did you think about how I would feel when I found out that you weren't dead? Did you think about how I would feel when I learned that there was another woman, with kids, in your life?"

"Where's my money, Lyn?" he asked, changing the subject.

"What money?"

"The money that was in the safe?"

"What money? I didn't take the money. Why do you think I went back to the house? I went to get the money," I lied. I'd long taken the money and had started to spend it to rebuild my life.

"You're lying," he spat. "Don't fuckin' lie to me."

"What reason would I have to lie? Unlike you, I don't have to lie. Have I ever lied to you before?" I quizzed. "Think about where I was when you found me? I was at the house, in the closet, at the damn safe. It was open and everything that was once in there was no longer there. Someone took the money and that box that you had in there." That box was the only reason I went back to the house. When Benedict told me that Logic was still alive, I didn't believe him. I knew that if it were true, everything that I would need to know would be in that box. Whenever Logic made big plans, he would stupidly write them down and put them inside that box. He must've known I'd eventually go back to the house to get the box so he moved it before I could get to it.

"Lyn, I love you. Don't play with me. I don't hit women and you know this. But, please don't think that I won't let Kosine get on your ass. You can see from how fragile Mercury looks that he doesn't play."

"Wow... You say you love me and then threaten to let another nigga put their hands on me? What kind of love is that? Who are you? What happened to the man I met and fell in love with?"

"He disappeared like the shit in that safe. I got the box, but all of my money was gone. I'm no fuckin' fool. You got my money and I want it back now," he aggressively spoke.

"Baby, I don't have the money. You've got to believe me. Maybe it was the men who I had come in and fix the house back up. It wasn't me." I forced myself to cry hopping it would make things more believable to him. That didn't work. He got closer to me and stared down into my eyes.

"You know I love you, don't you, Lyn? Everything I did was for you, baby."

"What happened? Why did you make me go through so much pain? Why couldn't you tell me what was up and take me with you?" I honestly wanted to know.

"It's a complicated situation. But I have a question for you," he said to me. He placed his hand in my head and began playing with my curls.

"What is it?" I curiously asked.

"How could you sleep with the enemy? You gave my pussy to the man that tried to kill me."

"What are you talking about?"

"You fucked that nigga, Day-Day. Why? That was my pussy," he yelled before going over to the wall and punching a big hole in it.

"I thought you were dead," I cried.

"Bitch, it ain't even been that long. Mufuckas wait years before they get over the person they really loved. Ain't no way you loved me and you were letting another nigga sniff around my shit. You have to pay for that shit, Lyn. You were unloyal to me."

"I was not unloyal! I stayed true to your ass until death did us part. You're the one who died. I still have fuckin' needs. My life had to go on. I was not about to be walking around with my hair all over my head like I was electrocuted, dressing raggedy as fuck, and being all depressed and shit. I was sick as hell over you at first. That was until I learned all that bullshit you did and that you had a whole other bitch. So, don't say shit to me about being loyal when you clearly don't have a loyal bone in your mufuckin' body," I spat. I was furious at that point. He was not about to talk to me crazy and get away with it. I demanded respect when we were together, and I was going to demand the same respect now.

"You're getting out of line, Lyn. Don't make me do this shit to you," he barked.

"Do what shit?" I quizzed.

"KOSINEEEEEEE!!" he yelled.

"What are you doing? What the hell are you calling him in here for?"

"You need to learn a lesson. What better way of you learning than to get a pro to teach you."

"Fine. If that's what you want to do, then go right ahead. I'm not about to beg you for shit. You wronged me and there were consequences behind it. Ain't that what you always used to say to me? I at least waited until I thought you were dead before I attempted to move on. You did the shit while I was still alive and have no remorse for it. If you can't forgive me then don't look for me to forgive your ass."

"What the fuck going on?" Kosine busted in the room wearing some red Ethicka boxers. I shook my head. Why the fuck did he have those good ass boxers on with that little ass dick? He pulled his hand from behind him displaying his gun before saying, "Nigga, fuck is you hollering for? What's going on?" He looked around the room, I'd assume to see if there was anything out of place.

"I need you to do me a favor," Logic finally spoke.

"A favor? What kind of favor?" Kosine questioned.

"I need you to give Lyn a Mercury special," he advised him.

"Mercury special? Fuck is that?"

"Teach her one of the lessons you be teaching Mercury's ass."

"Nigga, is you stupid?" Kosine asked him.

"What?" Logic faced him and asked, walking toward him.

"Don't walk up on me, bro. You dumb as hell if you think I'm going to beat Lyn. She not that type of chick. It's certain women you beat and she ain't it. She ain't wrong your ass. You foul as fuck for even wanting to do some dumb shit like that and then you're going to want to be with her later," Kosine explained. I grabbed my chest like I was clutching pearls or something. I was shocked. Why the fuck was Kosine taking up for me? Against Logic of all people.

"What you say to me, nigga?" Logic was angry as fuck. His nostrils flared up and down and his breathing increased and became heavy as hell.

"Pump yo brakes, big dawg. Let me explain something to you. When you got with Lyn, you knew she was the type of woman that you held on to. That's why you did that whole fake marriage shit. You had a first wife, but which one did you stay with? Which one did you take out in public? Who was at all events? Who was the one you made sure to have me check up on whenever you were gone? When you came out of hiding, it was because you were scared that another nigga was about to take her from you and there wouldn't be a chance for you to get her back. You never did that shit with Kazya or no other woman. Why would I beat her and you end up tarnishing her or losing her for good? What sense does that make?" Kosine explained. He finally spoke with some sense. I almost wanted to respect his ass, but I wasn't a fool. Kosine was up to something.

"I gave you an order," Logic roared.

"And you're not my mufuckin' boss. We work side by side, nigga. This ain't no street shit. This personal. You handle that yourself," Kosine retorted.

"Was it personal when you were running your dick in my bitch?" Logic asked out of nowhere.

When I heard those words flow from Logic's mouth, I knew it was over. Some shit was about to go down and it was not looking good for me. That's when I remembered that he was trying to kill me right before his supposed murder happened because he knew about what happened between me and Kosine. What was bothering me was why he was so mad about me being with Day-Day, yet he didn't seem quite angry about me sleeping with Kosine. If anything, that should've been what he was angry about. Kosine was almost like a brother to him and I was his wife. That was the most scandalous shit ever. I'd understand him wanting to murk me behind that because I was in the wrong. At the same time, there really wasn't shit he could say. He had a whole different bitch. A family. If I had a dick, I'd tell his ass to suck it.

## 4

## KOSINE

"What nigga?" I played dumb. Shit between Logic and I were already rocky. Things were really about to go left. How the fuck did he even find out?

"You didn't think I knew. I've known for a while. I'm surprised Lyn's cheating ass didn't mention it to you. Then Kazya told me what happened at the restaurant. I heard all about that and how selfish Lyn was when it came to giving her money to feed my kids," he announced.

"I'm glad you heard that. You should've also heard the keyword of those being YOUR KIDS. Got me fucked up! You cheated on me and got the next bitch pregnant yet didn't want me to have any kids. Wrong bitch!" Lyn snapped.

"Shut up. I'm not talking to you, Lyn."

"You don't have to be talking to me to be talking about me. Find somebody else to play with because it ain't me."

"Shut your dumb ass up. At least I fucked a bitch you ain't know. You fucked my mufuckin' cousin. You a trifling hoe."

Before I knew it, Logic was up on Lyn with his hands wrapped around her throat. He was choking the shit out of her. I was secretly in love with her. I wanted to save her. That would mean me giving away my feelings for her by going against him. I didn't know what to do. Then it dawned on me that Mercury was the key. I dashed out the room and darted down the hall to where Mercury was sleeping on the floor. Yanking her up by the arm, I pulled her back down the hall to where Logic and Lyn were. He was still choking her when I returned to the room.

"Look at this shit. Look at what the fuck you caused." Mercury was on the floor. I kicked her in the stomach causing her to scream out in pain.

"Please don't," Mercury pleaded with me not to hit her again.

"Apologize for all this shit you caused," I ordered.

"I'm sorry," she apologized, not knowing what the fuck I was talking about.

Logic heard the commotion and let Lyn go. He pushed her down on the bed and came over to where Mercury was. He picked her up off the floor and moved over to the bed with her. She was only wearing her bra and panties. I wondered what the fuck he was on. That nigga had never moved so crazy in his life. He snatched her panties off and pulled his dick out of the slit in his boxers. That nigga didn't give a fuck about Lyn and me standing in the room. He got in the bed with Mercury and climbed between her legs. She just laid there, not saying a word. The fact that she didn't put up a fight added to the rage that was growing inside of me.

Logic fumbled around at her opening for a while before finally saying, "Fuck it." He got up and stood before Lyn.

"That bitch ain't wet and her shit so tight I can't even get in," he barked.

"Nigga, I fucked her all night, so I know you a lie," I said. I'm not even sure the reason I said that dumb shit.

"Says a lot," Logic rebutted.

"What the fuck is that supposed to mean?"

"If you fucked her all night and I still can't get into her, there is clearly a difference in size. I ain't want the bitch no way. Both of y'all get the fuck out of here so I can deal with my wife," he ordered.

"Naw, fuck that shit. We 'bout to hash this out because I'm sick of you and your shit. All our lives, you've been walking around this bitch acting like you were better than me. You call me your right-hand when I'm actually supposed to be your partner. I never argued with you because my money was always right when it came down to that shit. Now, it's about respect," I chided.

"Ko, get the fuck out of my face. You fucked my bitch, and you want to talk to me about some mufuckin' respect. I don't respect you or shit about you. You can either play your part or get the fuck on down. I don't beg no bitch, so you know damn well I'm not about to beg no nigga."

Out the corner of my eyes, I could see Lyn standing behind me trying her best to regain control of her breathing. Her eyes were bloodshot red. Seeing her hurt, hurt me and I normally didn't give a fuck about anybody or anything. The feelings I had for Lyn were real. If she were to give me a chance, I knew I'd be a completely different person. I had to get Logic away from her. There was no way I could let him kill her.

"Logic, I'm sorry. I don't know how it happened or why. We were drinking. I'm sorry, baby. Please forgive me," Lyn's soft voice spoke. She was crying uncontrollably and begging Logic to forgive her. That threw me for a loop. She was popping shit to him a minute ago and now she was pleading with his ass for forgiveness. What the fuck was really going on?

***Whap...***

Logic hit Lyn in the mouth. My eyes grew wide as hell. I had to be seeing shit until...

***Whap...***

Logic hit her again. Lyn went flying back on the bed next to Mercury who still had yet to move. They both laid on the bed crying like some newborn babies. I'd seen enough. I ran up on Logic and pulled him away from her. I pushed him over into a corner and held him back.

"This ain't you, Logic. You don't hit women. Calm the fuck down, bro," I tried reasoning with him.

"Bro? You are not my fuckin' bro. You ain't shit to me. You fucked my bitch. You talking to me crazy. You're disrespecting my orders. Fuck you, Ko," he rattled off before pushing me off him.

"Nigga, don't push me." I pushed his ass back. Next thing I knew, we were rolling on the floor in a brawl. If you didn't know how close we were, you'd think we were two random ass nigga's fighting. I'm not even sure how long we were fighting before I heard footsteps coming up the stairs. We were being pulled apart by the niggas that worked for us.

"Get your fuckin' hands off me," I yelled at them when I'd gotten off the floor. Logic looked perfectly fine with his ugly ass smirk on his face while I had blood running from my nose and mouth. That nigga busted my shit.

"Y'all are brothers. What the fuck!! You can't be fighting like that. How the fuck you gonna lead us when you can't even get your shit together?" Damon, one of the workers, stated.

"I'ma see you, nigga," I said to Logic. I meant that shit. He was going to pay for fuckin' up my shit and for what he did to Lyn.

***RATATATATATAT... RATATATATATAT...***

Out of nowhere, bullets began flying through the house. Everyone in the room took cover but made it a point to start shooting back. I rushed over to the bed and pulled Lyn down to the floor. I left Mercury's dumb ass lying up there. I didn't give a fuck what happened to her at this point. She'd caused me more problems than she was worth. Had she not run her mouth about what happened between Lyn and I, Logic and I wouldn't be going through the rift that we were going through. We'd had problems before, but never this damn bad.

Once the shooting stopped, I had Damon untie Lyn. I moved around to make sure everyone was good before I rushed down the stairs.

"LOGICCCCCCC...." I called out to his punk ass.

"Fuck you calling my name for?" He ran downstairs panicked. That was until he saw the same thing I'd seen. Nayonni was gone. That bitch left and came back with the calvary trying to take us out. She was sending us a message about fucking with her.

"That bitch has got to die and her brother to," Logic roared.

"Everybody load up. We going to cause some problems," I announced.

It wasn't long before everyone was ready to go. We left the house, leaving Lyn and Mercury together. We left two men there to watch their asses. They couldn't eat, sleep, piss, or shit without one of those men being with their asses at all times. Logic and I had to come together at this point. But he'd better believe that I was not done with his ass yet.

## 5

## CORDE'

"Yo-Yo, where are you?" I called out to my sister when I'd reached her home. She was nowhere to be found. My nerves got the best of me as I noticed that her house was a mess. Someone had been there. Someone had taken my sister. I was going to tear up the whole state if something happened to her. Whomever had an issue with me needed to take the shit up with me, not her.

Taking my phone out, I continuously called her phone. Each time it went straight to voicemail. That wasn't like her at all. I tried calling Lyn to see if she was okay while I waited to see if Yo-Yo was going to call me back. When Lyn didn't answer either, my mind started to get the best of me. Some shit wasn't adding up.

Checking Yo-Yo's garage, I noticed that both of her vehicles were there. She wasn't the type to leave with anybody because she said when she was ready to go, she was going to leave on her own time. That was always understandable to me and it taught me to be the same damn way. I tried calling her phone one last time before I stepped outside and walked over to her neighbor's house. She lived next door to an older woman named Ms. Bertha. She was an old frisky ass cougar. If I went for older women, I'd give her ass the business. Age wasn't shit when you aged the way she did, like a fine wine. She was a true example of black not cracking.

***Knock... Knock... Knock...***

It seemed like I knocked on her door a hundred times before she finally answered.

"Why are you knocking on my door like that?" she asked me when she finally opened it.

"Hey to you too, Ms. Bertha," I greeted her.

"What I tell you about that Ms. shit? You call me Bertha or Sugar Momma," she commented before reaching out and grabbing at my ass.

"Ms. Bertha, I told you that I RESPECT MY ELDERS," I loudly spoke. I wanted her to know that the only way I viewed her was as an elder in hopes that she would let go of the thought that we'd ever be anything more than that.

"Damn. Fuck up a wet dream why don't you. What you want?" She caught an attitude.

"Have you seen my sister? I got a text from her and drove all the way here. When I got to her house, she was nowhere to be found and her house looks like someone tore it up," I expressed.

"That's because they did," she informed me.

"Say what?"

"Yeah. A few days ago, some men came in there and tore her house all the way up. I thought I heard her screaming. I looked out the window but didn't see her. Then her garage came up and some car I'd never seen before went jetting out of there, but I still didn't see her."

"You mean to tell me that you saw all of that and didn't think to call and let me know?"

"You know I don't get into other people's business. I know about y'all and what y'all do. I'm trying to stay alive."

"Let me get this straight... Every time you see me, you want me to drop this dick off into you and send your old ass to an early grave. Yet, when my sister could be in trouble, you don't say shit because you don't want to die? Get the fuck outta hea!" I wanted to knock her old ass out, but I couldn't find it in my heart to do so. "You know what, never mind..." It was best for me to walk away before I said or did something that I would regret later.

"I can't believe you're talking to me like that," she gasped.

"Well believe it with your twisted wig wearing ass," I barked before turning and walking away. The shit was unreal. My sister was nowhere to be found. For her to have seen something and not say anything pissed me off.

As I was walking away, I thought about the text that I'd received. If Ms. Bertha had seen something, she may have been able to identify someone who was involved with Yo-Yo's disappearance. That caused me to turn and go back to her home. She was still standing in her doorway with her mouth gapped open. Since I needed something from her, I had no choice but to be nice to her.

"I'm not saying I was wrong for going off on you, but I'm going to say that I was wrong for what I said. I didn't mean to say what I said to you."

"About dropping dick in me or about my wig being twisted?"

"Oh naw, I meant what I said about your wig being twisted. It has been like that for years. The shit fucked up now. Matter fact..." I leaned in and turned her wig to where her part was in the center of her forehead and pulled it down a little to hide the fact that she didn't have any edges and then proceeded to speak again. "Like I was saying, I shouldn't have said all that shit I said about dying and putting my dick in the mix. My bad about that. You have to understand where I'm coming from. My sister is all that I have. If you know anything, please tell me." This time I was sure to talk to her in a gentle tone. Her facial expression softened, and she finally closed her mouth.

"You a messy bitch," she said to me. She smacked her lips and rolled her eyes. I chose not to respond to her remark. If I would've said anything else wrong to her, she wouldn't help me.

She was a bitter old coon, so I knew she would've been a bitch.

"Will you please tell me everything that you saw," I requested, damn near pleading with her. I wasn't the type of man that begged. However, when it came down to my sister, I was willing to do damn near anything to find out where she was and get her back home safely.

"All I know is that some fine specimen of a man showed up and knocked on her door. Hell, he was almost as fine as you. But you know I'd never pick another man over you, boo," she stated and reached her wrinkled ass hand out to touch my face. I smacked it away.

"Quit the bullshit and tell me what you know."

"What do I get out of this?" she asked, licking her lips and winking. She even had the nerve to try to shake her ass a little. All that did was show that she needed a hip replacement with her knock-kneed ass. "Huh? What you gonna give me?" she asked again. Irritated, I pulled my gun out and aimed it at her. Placing it on the center of her forehead, I pushed her inside of her house. Never being one to kill an innocent person, I hated to have to start today.

"Wait... I'll tell you whatever you want to know."

"I know the fuck you will and It's sad that I have to do this. All you had to do was give me the information I asked you for. You couldn't do that. See where that got you. TALK DAMNIT!" I found myself raising my voice. I was agitated as hell and she wasn't making shit no better.

Ms. Bertha stood in front of me not saying a word. The expression on her face showed that she was scared. I didn't blame her. I was a dangerous man whether she knew it or not. Since she acted like she didn't want to talk, I figured I'd have to make her. Thankfully the silencer stayed on my gun. I aimed it down at the floor and began shooting. Ms. Bertha moved as fast as she could trying to avoid the bullets as I shot at her feet. It almost seemed like she was breakdancing. I wanted to laugh,

I couldn't. If I did, she may have thought I was playing with her.

Three minutes into me shooting at her feet, she looked exhausted. Deciding to give her a break, I put my gun away and took a seat on her couch.

"Why would you do that to me?" She was exhibiting a hard time breathing.

"You got asthma?" I queried. She nodded her head.

"Where is your rescue inhaler?" She pointed to her dining room table. I stood from where I was sitting and walked to the table. Picking the inhaler up, I walked toward her. Acting as if I was about to hand It to her, when she reached her hand out for it, I yanked mine back. "Not until you give me what I came here for."

"I can't breathe," she announced.

"How do you think I feel not knowing where my sister is?"

"All... I... Know... Is... That... Some... Man... Took... Her..." She managed to get out in between breaths. I handed her the inhaler and let her take two puffs before snatching it back from her.

"Have a seat. If you don't finish telling me everything you saw, your ass will be dancing all the way to the grave and I mean that shit," I warned her. Very cautiously she moved over to the couch. She took her time sitting down. I kept glancing at my watch so she'd see that I wanted her to hurry up.

"I'm sorry, Day-Day. I told you everything that I know. A man knocked on the door and your sister opened it. I saw that much because I was standing outside. Out of nowhere, a whole bunch of other cars pulled up. It scared me so I ran inside the house. She had to have known him or she wouldn't have opened the door, right?" The mention of Yo-Yo knowing the man made me think back to the text that I received. I took my phone out and pulled up a photo I had of Logic and Kosine from when I had them being watched. I showed the picture to Ms. Bertha.

"Is this the man?" I asked, pointing at Kosine.

"No," she replied.

"Damn!" I snarled. I thought for sure it had to have been him.

"It was the other man," she acknowledged, pointing to Logic. I pounded my fist down on the table. When we were at dinner with Lyn's parents, the man that was with them told us that Logic was alive. I thought it was some sick joke. Apparently, it wasn't. He had faked his death and went into hiding. For him to have come out to pay my sister a visit meant something was wrong.

"Did you hear anything?" I asked Ms. Bertha hoping she could give me some information that could either lead me to where they were or help me figure out what they were planning to do.

"I thought I heard her scream, but it was very brief. I peeked through the blinds and saw the men inside her house tearing things up. I wanted to call the police, but she always told me to never do that."

"Thank you," I told her and left her home.

If Logic and Kosine had my sister, there was a reason why. The only problem was that I didn't know the reason. We never beefed with them. The only thought that came to my mind was that this had something to do with Lyn. They were coming after me because I started dealing with her. That was the only thing that made sense. I did the only thing I could think to do. I picked the phone up and dialed Lyn's number once again. She had to be the answer to getting my sister back.

# 6
## MERCURY

"I know I'm probably the last person you want to talk to or deal with right now, but we need each other," I expressed to Lyn. We were still on the bed that she'd shared with Logic the night before.

"Why are you talking to me? I don't fuck with bitches like you," she snapped. I knew that was the anger and hurt talking. It was my fault. I pulled her into some bullshit because I was mad at her about something that she couldn't control.

"Look, I need to tell you something." If I was going to get her to work with me, I had to start by being truthful with her. Plus, I needed to get the shit off my conscious. Living with the guilt was driving me crazy.

"What could you possibly have to tell me? That you ain't shit?" she spat.

"You're not about to keep talking to me crazy. I deal with enough of that from Kosine. I would expect you to understand."

"Expect me to understand? You tried to shame me for something that was not my fault. We weren't best friends or no shit like that, but we talked enough times for you to know me. You know damn well that Kosine isn't my type and even if he was, I'd never go after someone else's man. That's not even my character."

"I know and I'm sorry. I was tired of him always putting his hands on me. I couldn't take my anger out on him, so I lashed out at you. I'm sorry about that. I wish you could understand where I'm coming from." I really did wish she understood what I was saying. They say hurt people hurt people and that's exactly what I did.

"I'd never be able to understand because I don't want to. You wronged me and now you have to deal with your ac-"

"He drugged you," I blurted out, halting her from finishing her statement. "Kosine put something in the wine. That was the only way he could get you to sleep with him. You weren't drunk. You didn't even drink the whole glass," I explained.

"How long have you known that?" she asked me.

"It's been a few months. I should've told you when I learned the truth, but I didn't. I was fucked up about the fact that I was trying to be the best woman I could be for him and all he wanted was you."

"He could want me all he wanted but I've never wanted him and never will." She stood firm behind that.

"I see where you're coming from. I can't do anything but respect what you're saying and your feelings about things. All I'm saying is right now, we need each other to get out of here. After that, we can go our own separate ways."

Lyn grew silent. She had to be thinking about what I suggested. The need to think about things, especially when it came to me was understandable. However, she needed to take into consideration that we were pushed for time. The guys ran out of here trying to find out what the fuck had happened. We didn't know where they went or when they'd be returning. It was our best bet to move as quickly as possible to do what we could to get the hell out of there.

"Fine. Let's get out of here. And just so you know, I'm not going to walk away when it's done. I still owe you an ass whooping. You're not avoiding that," she remarked. I couldn't even be mad. I'd done more than enough to her for her to want to put her hands on me. With any luck, if we worked well together, she'd change her mind. I didn't think I could afford for anyone else to put their hands on me. Kosine had done more than enough damage.

"Bet," I replied. There was really nothing more I could say. We both struggled with getting up from the bed, me more than her. I limped toward the window, holding my side from where Kosine had viciously kicked me.

"You need to put some clothes on," Lyn informed me, reminding me that I was half dressed. Instead of responding to her, I poked my head out the door of the room and peeked out in the hallway. When I didn't see anyone, I moved as fast as I could across to the room that Kosine had been keeping me in. Locating my clothes, I quickly put them and my shoes on. I briefly searched the room for anything I could potentially use as a weapon in case he came back. There wasn't anything in there.

"Come on. We have to try to get out of here." Lyn's head popped inside the room I was in. She turned to leave, and I was right on her heels. We took our time heading for the stairs until we heard some movement downstairs.

"Someone is coming," Lyn announced.

"Maybe we can hide in the attic," I suggested.

"They'll find us," she quipped.

"We can pull the string in. That would be the last place they'd think to look. It may buy us some time to come up with a plan to get the hell out of here," I concluded. The words coming out of my mouth sounded good, but I was scared as hell. I knew that by us trying to get away, that was like a death wish if Logic and Kosine were to find us.

"I don't know about all of that. You trying to run up the stairs like them dumb ass folks do in the movies. If anything, we need to be downstairs. At least if we need to go out of a window, we'll have a better chance for survival," she advised me. It made a lot of sense.

"I get that. I'm nervous that if we try to go down the stairs, we are going to get caught," I remarked.

"Mercury, if they come up here looking for us and don't see us coming down the stairs, the attic is going to be the first place they think to check," she commented.

"If we go down the stairs and they don't see us, then they are still going to check the attic," I argued.

"No, they'll check the basement first. I'm trying to think and you're fuckin' with my brain cells," she fussed.

"I'm telling you that the attic is our best bet right no-"

My words were halted when I started to hear movement above me. Someone was in the attic. I thought for sure that the only people in the house were Lyn, me, and the two fools they had stay there with us. I was scared. Someone had heard us.

"Someone is coming," I blurted out, frantically.

"Chill out, Merc. You're going to get us caught," Lyn advised me.

"Get us caught? We're already caught. You don't hear that?" I questioned her. She threw a finger over her mouth to motion for me to be quiet. Lyn leaned over the top of the stair railing to see if she saw anyone. When she didn't, she let out a sigh of relief.

***Creeeeeeaaaaaakkkk....***

A loud creaking noise could be heard above us. Lyn removed the finger from her mouth and pointed up. She wasn't telling me anything that I didn't know. Somebody was in the attic. The same damn attic that I was trying to convince her to go inside of. Lyn started walking along the sides of the wall slowly, she went in the direction that the attic door was located. For a minute, I thought she was going to open it. She didn't. She ducked off to the room that was closest to the attic door. I damn near took off running behind her. There was no way I was going to get left behind. As I entered the room, I bumped right into her.

"Damn, watch where you're going, bitch!" she spat, her tone

laced with agitation. I knew she was still pissed at me. She could've at least let the shit go long enough for us to figure out what the hell our next move should be.

"Get under the bed and be quiet," she instructed.

"Wait... That would leave you unprotected," I told her.

"Don't act like you care now. Get under the bed and don't say shit," she ordered. Not wanting to argue with her and make things worse between us, I did what she said. I got far enough under the bed to where I couldn't be seen but I was still able to look from under it to see what the hell was going on.

There was a small ass TV sitting on top of the dresser. It couldn't have been any bigger than 40-inches. Lyn went behind the TV and snatch the cord from behind it. I was prepared for her to wrap the cord around her hands so that she could use it to strangle someone if she had to, but that wasn't what she did. Lyn's crazy ass picked up the whole fuckin' TV. She always looked to be strong, but damn. I wasn't sure what the hell she was planning on doing with it. As long as she wasn't doing it to me, I didn't care. Holding the TV, Lyn moved closer to the opened door and placed her back against the wall. We played the waiting game at that point.

## 7

# NAYONNI (YO-YO)

There was a small window located in the attic, so I was able to see everything that transpired outside once the smoke had cleared from all of the shooting. I noticed that Logic and Kosine had left and took what I would assume most of the crew with them. I also noticed that I didn't spot the two women that they had at the house when they left. I knew about the one that Kosine stayed beating. I wasn't sure who the other one was yet, but I knew her ass didn't want to be there. That was evident by the amount of hollering she had done. Plus, I'd managed to put my ear to the floor and tried to hear as much as I could from where I was. It all sounded muffled, but I was able to hear enough to learn that things between Kosine and Logic wasn't where they needed them to be. That worked out in my favor. Killing them would be easier if their heads weren't in the game.

Although they were gone and I felt that the women were still in the house, that also meant that he had to have left some men behind to watch them. They weren't crazy enough to leave and not leave anyone there with them. Too much freedom would give them a chance to run. With them gone, I decided it was the perfect time for me to try to get out of the house. Slowly, I moved over to the attic door and pushed it down a little so I could peek down. When I didn't see or hear anything, I pushed it open a little further. Silently praying to myself for a few minutes, I pushed it the rest of the way open and climbed out of the attic. I still had the nigga's cell phone from last night. I couldn't use it because my silly ass didn't have my brother's number.

When I left out of the attic, I wasn't empty handed. There was an old cane up there. It wasn't much of a weapon, but something was better than nothing. I had it clutched hard in my hands as I stepped off the last step. There was no conversation to be heard around me so that told me that the men who worked for Logic were not up there. That was when I decided I'd look for the woman I knew had been getting her ass beat by Kosine. I didn't know her or anything about her other than the fact that her name was Mercury. I felt bad for her. Nobody deserved to get their ass beat the way he'd been handling her. When granted the opportunity, he was going to be the first person I put out of their misery.

"Kosine's bitch," I said above a whisper. I went from room to room checking to see if I could find her. I started on the right side of the hall checking the rooms and made my way back toward the attic door. I was strategically moving that way so that I would end up back by the attic in the event that I would have to run back up the stairs.

"Kosine's bitch. I know you hear me. Where are you?" I called out again. "I'm not here to hurt you. I'm trying to get out of here too. You knew I was downstairs, and you didn't try to help me. I'm not going to do you like that since I know he been beating your ass," I explained. I wasn't talking loudly but if she was upstairs, she should've been able to hear me because it was so quiet up there.

My right foot was halfway inside the last room when I glanced up and saw a reflection in the mirror. I couldn't tell if it were a man or a woman, but I raised the cane over my head and was getting ready to swing. Whomever it was raised something up in the air but didn't get too far.

"Wait..." The bitch I'd been calling came rolling from under the bed, stopping us from hitting each other.

"Were you about to hit me in the head with a fuckin' TV?" I asked the woman. I couldn't help but giggle because that was some shit I would've done. "Who are you?" I asked her.

"I'm Lyn. I'm Logic's w-"

"Wife," I interrupted her. The minute she said her name, I knew exactly who she was.

"Something like that," she replied. I knew all about her. Day-Day talked about her non-stop whenever we did talk. All I could do was embrace her. I wrapped my arms around her as tight as I could. It had nothing to do with whether or not I knew her. It had everything to do with the fact that my brother was feeling her. That was something I'd never known him to do. She made him happy and he deserved that. It was my duty to protect her until we could get to him.

"You know her?" Kosine's bitch asked. That reminded me of the seriousness of the situation we were in. I pulled away from her.

"No. She knows my brother. I'm Nayonni," I introduced myself.

"Your brother? Who is your brother?" she asked me.

"I'm not sure if you know him as Day-Day or Corde'," I expressed.

"Oh, my God! Where is he? He needs to find us," she cried.

"It's okay. I got us. I need to call him."

"Call him? How? Is there a phone here?" she quizzed.

I briefly explained to them what happened last night. I also dropped my head when I told her how embarrassed I was that I didn't know his number and couldn't call him.

"Give me that damn phone," she advised me.

Handing her the phone, I stood there and watched as she keyed in some numbers. She placed the phone on speaker and handed it back to me. Not before she turned it down so that it wouldn't be too loud.

"If you have my sister, your ass is dead," Day-Day hollered through the phone when he answered.

"Day-Day, it's me," I cried. Tears ran down my face. That was not normal for me. Not in front of other people. It was something that couldn't be helped though. I was thankful to hear his voice. I felt tough and acted that way, but I was torn up on the inside.

"Where are you? What the fuck happened?" He started firing off question after question.

"Now is not the time to ask questions. You need to get to us ASAP," I informed him.

"Us? Who the hell is us?" he asked.

"Baby, I'm here too," Lyn spoke. Her voice was trembling.

"Who did this shit?" Rage could be heard illuminating in his voice as he spoke.

"Logic and Kosine," I hollered through the phone.

"Baby, are you okay? Did he put his hands on you?" he asked Lyn.

"I don't want to talk about all of that right now. We need you to come get us," she reiterated to him.

"Where are you?"

Call me crazy, but I started to feel a little jealous. For the first time, my brother seemed more concerned about someone other than me. There was a mixture of jealousy and joy in my heart. Jealous because he was putting someone else first. Joy because he had finally found happiness and that was the one thing I'd always wanted for him. He deserved it. Yeah, we did some fucked up shit when it came to assassinating people. That was our job. Yet, he always had a big heart and would go out of his way to help anyone that he could. That was one thing I admired about him. I was a different story. If you couldn't help me, I wasn't going to help you. That reminded me of Kosine's bitch. She could've helped me but opted not to.

"I'ma need for y'all to deal with that love shit later. We need to get the hell out of here," I expressed, pulling the phone away from her.

"Sorry," she apologized.

"Don't be sorry, hoe; be careful," I joked, trying to make light of the situation.

"Don't get fucked up, Yo-Yo," Day-Day muttered.

"Damn. I'm playing. Chill out, bro. I'm about to send you the location. You need to get here as fast as you can."

"Where are Logic and Kosine now?"

"Somebody started shooting at this dump that they have us in and they took off after them," I informed him.

"That meant they left in a hurry. How many guys are there with you?" he asked.

"There are two," Kosine's bitch chimed in. I glanced up at her, rolled my eyes, and then refocused my attention back on the phone.

"Yo-Yo?" he called out my name.

"Yeah, bro?" I replied.

"I know damn well you're not on this phone telling me that there are two niggas there guarding you and you ain't knocked them the fuck out yet? Fuck you on?" he grunted.

"Day-Day, don't start that shit with me. I didn't know how many niggas were here. And even if I do fuck them up, who's to say that we have a way out of here?" I quizzed.

"Fuck all that. You better man the fuck up and handle that shit. What kinda phone you on?" he asked.

"An iPhone."

"Send me the mufuckin' location. I'm on my way. If them niggas touch you or Lyn, I'm blowing up the whole fuckin' state," he roared.

"I'm here too," Kosine's bitch blurted out.

"Who the fuck is that?" Day-Day asked.

"That's Kosine's bitch," I replied.

"My name is Mercury," she had the nerve to correct me.

"I don't give a fuck what your name is. What I do give a fuck about is the fact that you knew I was tied to a fuckin' chair and you did nothing to try and help me. I should leave your bitch ass here," I fussed.

"He would've killed me. What was I supposed to do?" she whined.

"You can't be a scary bitch all your life. That nigga smokes, don't he?" I quizzed.

"Yeah. What does that have to do with anything?" she curiously asked.

"The first time he put his hands on me would've been the last time. He would've fallen asleep and woke up to the damn bed being on fire. Fuck all that! Ain't enough money or love in the world to make me stay with a man that's beating me," I expressed.

"You can't judge me. None of you can. Until you've walked a day in my shoes, you'll never know what it was like," she justified.

"Mercury, shut your bitch ass up," Day-Day rattled off through the phone. "You ain't got two words to say to me. You tried to handle Lyn and I'm not with that shit. Now, I'm hearing you didn't help my sister. You've burned your bridge with me. Matter fact leave that bitch there," Day-Day ordered.

"No. Please don't. If you leave me, he's going to kill me," she pleaded with us.

"We can deal with her later. Right now, we need to find a way out of here," Lyn reasoned. She took the phone. "Corde', I know that you don't care for Mercury. Trust me, I don't either. We can't leave her though. We all know what Kosine is capable of and I'm not about to be walking around here with someone's blood on my hands. He will kill her for sure," Lyn assured him.

"They could've killed me, and she did nothing," I chimed in.

"Then beat her ass after we get out of this shit. Right now, we need to find a way out of here. All of us," Lyn commented.

"Fine," I agreed even though I didn't want to.

"Sis, I'm leaving that on you. I'm not fuckin' with Mercury. You get one chance to disrespect my girl and it's a wrap with me. Her chance came and went," Day-Day told me. Respect was the only thing that could be given. Nobody could fault him for feeling the way that he felt. Lyn was his woman and he had to protect her at all costs.

Sending Day-Day the location, I ended the call to preserve the battery. We didn't know when we'd have to use the phone again or if there was an iPhone charger anywhere to be found in the house.

"We need to find something we can use to protect ourselves," I told the women.

"There's got to be a safe around here. I'm sure it would have something we could use," Lyn voiced.

"Wait... I know where it is," Mercury blurted out.

"How? Where is it?" I quizzed.

"When we first got here, the men kept walking into the room at the end of the hall."

"The room Logic had me in?"

"No, the room next to it. I'm not sure what they kept going in there for but there were times I saw them going in with things that they never came back out with," she explained.

"Let's go then," I stated. I left out of the room first and Lyn was right behind me. I turned to see where Mercury was, but she was nowhere to be found.

"Lyn, I'm telling you that if she doesn't help us do shit, she's going to get left here."

"I agree," Lyn remarked, and we kept walking.

"Do you know where they would keep it?" I whispered to Lyn.

"If I know Logic, he's going to keep it somewhere that he doesn't think anyone would look. I'd say try the closet or a secret spot cut out under a bed or something. He thinks he's being strategic, but I always figure him out," Lyn yapped.

It wasn't long before we found ourselves walking inside the

room that Mercury had told us about. Still, she was nowhere in sight. Lyn and I moved around as quickly and quietly as possible to see what we could find. It took us roughly five minutes before she thought it would be best to move the dresser around. It was heavy when we tried to move it. We needed Mercury's help even though we knew she was battered and bruised. With the three of us working together, it wouldn't have been that hard for us to move.

"Let me go get this ditzy broad," I told Lyn. As I was getting ready to leave out of the room, Mercury came prancing inside.

"Y'all need to keep it down. If I could hear you down the hall, I can only imagine what they hear downstairs," she commented. That's when I took the time to look around. I dropped down and looked under the bed, opened the closet door to look inside, and even looked behind the dresser.

"What are you looking for?" Mercury finally asked.

"I'm looking for the bitch you talking to cuz I know damn well you wasn't talking to me and her," I said, pointing between Lyn and me.

"We can't do this right now," Lyn chimed in.

"Fine. You need to get her because one more wrong word and I'ma bop her ass in the mouth," I advised them both.

The remainder of the time searching the room was done in silence. We moved around as quietly as possible trying to find the safe. Lyn and I finally lifted the dresser and moved it out of the way. It was sitting on top of a rug. Mercury tiptoed over and moved the rug out of the way. I looked over at her and shook my head. Of all the ways she could've helped, the one thing she thought to do was move a mufuckin' rug?

"Don't," Lyn stopped me before I opened my mouth to call Mercury on her bullshit. Clamping my mouth shut, I watched as Lyn dropped down to her knees and lifted the wooden planks from the floor. There was a safe right where she said it would be. Somewhere Logic knew people wouldn't think to look for it.

Lyn punched in a few codes before the safe finally beeped.

She opened it up and my mouth dropped. It was full of money, there were two guns, two sets of IDs, and two cell phones. I later learned that one phone belonged to Mercury and the other one belonged to Lyn.

"I won't be needing this," Lyn quipped. She took her phone and stepped inside the bathroom. I witnessed her dropping it in the toilet. Glancing over at Mercury, I waited to see if she was going to do the same thing, but she didn't.

"I'm holding on to mine. I have an idea," she told us as she stuck the phone down in her bra. "Plus, it has pictures of my daughter. I have to keep them since I don't know if I'll ever see her again," she added.

"Whatever. Let's get the fuck out of here," I told the ladies as I took both of the guns. We headed down the stairs in search of the two men left behind. If Logic was mad before, he was really going to be mad when he came back to an empty house and dead workers.

# 8

# KOSINE

Once the shooting subsided, Logic and I took off in search of the person responsible. When we got down the stairs, we noticed that Yo-Yo was gone. Witts was laid out on the floor, unresponsive. I ran over to him and kicked him until he came to.

"What happened?" I asked him.

"That bitch knocked me out," he admitted, embarrassment was all over his face.

"We know that much. How when she was tied to a damn chair? That doesn't make any sense," Logic commented. I agreed with him. How could someone who wasn't restrained get their ass kicked by someone who was? With us questioning him, he finally broke down and told us what really happened. That angered me.

***Pow...***

Without warning, I swiftly turned my gun on him and sent a bullet sailing between his eyes. He dropped like a damn fly. That's when I told Logic that Yo-Yo had to be behind the shooting, and that we needed to find her as quickly as possible.

"Yo two stay here and watch them," I told two of the workers. "And clean this shit up," I barked out orders. I watched out the corner of my eyes at Logic slapping himself on the forehead, dropping his head, and shaking it. The one thing he didn't do was open his mouth and speak on anything. That was the best thing for him to do. We split the crew up and decided we would go two separate ways. While he rode in the car with one of the workers, I got in my truck and rode alone. There were members of the crew trailing me.

***Ring... Ring... Ring...***

The sound of my phone ringing fucked with my nerves. I wasn't expecting anyone to call me. I needed a fix bad, but I knew this wasn't the time for that to happen.

"Yeah?" I answered without checking to see who was calling.

"Did we get him?" my boy, Chico asked.

"No, nigga. Why the fuck are you calling me?" I grunted. He knew damn well that he wasn't supposed to call me. All communication that we had was only supposed to happen if I called him or we met up somewhere. I'd hired him, but something had me feeling as though I really couldn't trust his ass.

"Aye, I'm tired of this shit. You told me that killing Logic was going to be easy. We've tried several times and each time has been unsuccessful. I'm about to get the fuck out of dodge before he catches on to what's going on. I don't need that nigga coming after me or my family," Chico whined.

"Nigga, shut your punk ass up. I told you that it was all going to happen in due time. You keep busting moves on your own and you keep failing. I'm sick of that shit."

"Then you need to give me direction on what to do. You told me that we were supposed to handle him at the house, but you changed your mind at the last minute. Either you want him dead or not," he fussed.

To some it would seem fucked up that I was going after Logic. Nobody could ever understand the reason why. I was tired of being in his shadow. He told me that we were going to be working side-by-side, but somewhere along the way, he got the big head. He started barking out orders and thinking I was supposed to just follow them. This wasn't a damn nine to five. I wasn't getting paid enough to ride his fuckin' balls and do whatever he wanted. He needed to learn to share. The same way he'd shared Lyn with me. Despite it being unvoluntary, it still happened.

Locked up in prison I was miserable having to do what a mufucka told me to do. I was a grown man. I didn't need anyone telling me when to eat, sleep, or shit. I was in there for some domestic violence, attempted murder shit. Had the bitch I was fuckin' with at the time did what I told her to do, it wouldn't have ended with me trying to beat the fuck out of her. If I must be truthful, no woman on this earth stood a chance with me and my hands. My mother wasn't shit and every woman I've encountered since then turned out to be the same way. My father used to beat her ass to get her in line so why not follow in his footsteps? Lyn was the only woman I ever came across that I never felt the need to hit. I watched how she was with Logic and I wanted that. That's why I had to get him out the way. That, mixed with the fact that he thought he was my damn daddy or some shit. I wasn't with all that. Therefore, I had to send a message to him.

"Nigga, are you there?" Chico grunted. "You need to tell me what to do? Are we killing him or not? Shit is getting too hot. It's only a matter of time before he finds out who's behind this."

"Stop being scary. That nigga not going to find out shit. I run this," I commented.

"You run this? If you so-called run this, then why the fuck won't you walk up to him and take him out yourself? You're so big and bad," Chico remarked.

"Fuck you! I paid you to do a job and you'd better do it. I'd kill hm if I wasn't trying to get his bitch. She'd never forgive me if she found out that I was behind any of this shit with Logic."

"She'll never forgive you if she found out how you got her in bed either. Either way, you're fucked my nigga," Chica stated and chuckled.

"Chico, I swear I'll kill you if that shit ever gets out," I warned him.

"I'm not the one that's going to tell her. You don't think Mercury is going to tell her what the hell you did? She may already know."

When he said that, I started thinking. Lyn had been acting different with me lately. I wondered if Mercury had already told her what was up and she didn't say anything to me about it yet. But who the hell told Mercury?

"I'm going to help you one more time. After that, you're on your own. I can't keep putting my family in danger. Give me a few days to get them out of dodge and we'll go after that nigga full force. Cool?"

"Aight. Bet," I told him and ended the call without another word being spoken between us. There was no reason for either of us to say anything more. It was understood what I needed him to do. He needed to hurry up and make that shit happen.

Having Logic think Yo-Yo and Day-Day were after him was my cover for my shady misdoings. They were the first people who came to mind. When I met with Day-Day, I really did want him to work with me. He was good at what he did. When he turned me down, it made sense for me to tell Logic that they were after him. Then when he decided to get with Lyn, that made it even better. All I had to do was convince Logic that getting rid of him was Day-Day's way to get with Lyn and that gave him another reason to believe me. Things were falling into place for me. I couldn't wait for the day that Logic was finally out of the way and I was running things.

There were a few loose ends that I needed to take care of. If Chico was getting scared, there was a chance that he could snitch and that was something I couldn't allow to happen. He told me he was going to try to kill Logic one more time before he got out of dodge. That wasn't our original agreement and certainly not what I paid him for. There was no trying involved. He had a job to do and that was to make sure Logic was dead.

There was no turning back from that. If he agreed to kill Logic, he was going to have to work until he made sure Logic had taken his last breath. To make sure that happened, I placed another call.

"Yo," my nigga Sleezy answered.

"You remember that shit we talked about a few months back?" I asked, saying as little as I had to over the phone.

"Yeah. What about it?" he muttered. The sound of him exhaling let me know he was smoking on some good shit. The fact that he started damn near coughing up a lung out of nowhere confirmed what I was already thinking.

"We need to make that shit happen. I need all three of those situations handled ASAP," I instructed him.

"Word," he responded and hung the phone up. A small smile crept across my face. If nothing else, things were really about to work out the way I wanted them to. It was only a matter of time. Logic might've thought things were rough when he had to go into hiding the first time. He definitely wasn't expecting what was about to happen. The south had better brace themselves because there was about to be a new nigga in charge. One that was going to take what belonged to him and that was these mufuckin' streets.

## 9

## EVELYN (LYN)

The men had been gone for a while. Mercury coming to me and asking for help was the last thing I expected. Knowing how she was, I knew that meant I'd be the one doing all the work. Nayonni being there was a blessing. She was able to do the things I'd never in a million years think to do. Prime example, when it came down to taking care of the fools Logic and Kosine left to watch us, we left that shit to Yo-Yo. She was trained to go, and we weren't. I knew when to stay in my lane and that was a time for me to do so.

Nayonni had both guns in her hands. She carried them with pride. I stood behind her. Mercury stayed upstairs. She wanted to stay out of dodge. I saw then why Nayonni wanted to leave her ass. Even though I agreed with her reasoning, my heart wouldn't let me do it.

"You think we need to go check on those bitches?" I heard one of the men asking the other while we were making our way down the stairs.

"Naw. They're straight. If I go up there, I'm running my dick in one of them hoes. Got us sitting around this bitch like we some babysitters or some shit," the other man fussed.

"Shole do. I'm sick of the shit. Logic used to be so much

better than he is now. He is letting Kosine make too many decisions and it's fuckin' shit up. I can't stand it. I'm thinking about dipping on them."

"You're talking crazy, Butta. We get paid good and Logic ain't never done us dirty."

"He hasn't yet. Think about all the stuff that went down when he went into hiding and didn't tell us. Hell, every time you look up now, somebody shooting at us. I didn't get in this game to die. I wanted to secure a bag to take care of my family. I got enough to walk away," Butta announced.

"You ain't got enough to walk away."

"How you know what I got?"

"If you did then you would've been walked away. Shit, we still at the bottom of the barrel trying to get to where them niggas at."

"Man, fuck all that. Go check on them hoes. I ain't got time for this shit," Butta told him. As soon as the other man got up to head for the stairs, Nayonni pulled the gun out she had behind her back and shot him right in the head. Butta stood up and was preparing to shoot her while she wasn't looking. There was no way I could let that go down like that. Snatching the other gun from behind her, I closed my eyes and squeezed the trigger.

***Pow... Pow... Pow... Pow...***

I kept shooting until I couldn't shoot anymore.

***Click... Click...***

The clicking of the gun let me know that I'd ran out of bullets. Yet, I could still hear shooting.

***Pow... Pow... Pow...***

Opening my eyes, I saw Nayonni shooting at Butta's ass. His body hit the floor hard. Just like that, he was gone. They both were.

"Thank you," Nayonni thanked me and removed the gun from my hands. I was trembling. "You didn't kill him but I'm glad to know you had my back unlike some hoes," she added, peering up the stairs at Mercury who stood there like she'd seen a ghost. Tears were streaming down her face.

"We have to get out of here," I told her.

"Get their guns. I'm going to call Day-Day back to see where he's at. He shouldn't be too far out," Nayonni stated. I ran to both men and took the guns from them. I hated that they had to die. It was either them or us. Luckily for me, I didn't have to catch my first body.

"Mercury, come on. We have to try to find a way out of here," I told her.

"They are going to kill us. We can't leave," she whined. My eyes bucked at her saying that.

"Is that why you've been holding back and not helping? How the hell you come to me saying we need to work together to end up doing this? God blessed us with someone that could help us and you still ain't do shit. We could leave you but we aren't. Don't start that dumb shit," I fussed.

"We don't know her. How do we know she's not really working with them?"

"Are you out of your mind? She's Corde's sister. She wouldn't do anything to hurt us. She's trying to get out of here like we are. What are you talking about?"

"All I'm saying is that it's a coincidence that she ended up here. How was she able to get free when they were here? It's not adding up. If you ask me, something isn't right. I don't trust her."

"You have got to be shittin' me right now."

"I'm giving you my opinion."

"Keep your thoughts to yourself, Mercury. You sound real dumb. I swear people get on my nerves. You haven't learned that opinions are like assholes? Everyone got one but some of those mufuckas stank. And right now, yours smelling foul as fuck," I shouted. Mercury had worked my last nerve.

"If you want to stay here, that's on you. I'm getting the hell out of here," I told her and walked off in search of Nayonni who was standing at the backdoor trying to open it.

"What's wrong?"

"It's jammed or something. We're going to have to go out of the front door," she advised me.

"How far away is your brother?"

"He said that he's maybe an hour away."

"We can't wait that long. They may be back before then."

"I know. That's why we have to go. NOW! There's a car outside. Check to see if they have keys on them," she told me.

Dashing back over to the lifeless bodies lying on the floor, I checked them both to see if I could find a set of keys. There was nothing. We searched the entire downstairs and didn't find a thing. Of course, Mercury stood there while we did all the searching. I was over her shit. There was no way I was going to push for her to leave again either. I'm not sure what it was, but something was keeping her there. For some reason, I felt it was more so her being jealous of Nayonni and her strength than it was of her being scared that Kosine was going to kill her if he found her.

"There's a coded keypad on the door. We can't get out," Mercury announced.

"Like hell if we can't," Nayonni remarked. She took the gun she was carrying and smashed out one of the front windows. She climbed out of it and ran toward the driveway where we saw the car parked. Glancing back at Mercury, I shrugged my shoulders and took off after Nayonni. She was not about to leave me.

We got outside and Nayonni busted out the window to the car to get inside of it. She got inside and did some shit with the wires under the steering wheel and the car crank right up. She unlocked the door and I hopped on the passenger's side. Nayonni began backing out of the driveway when we heard someone yelling. We looked up to find Mercury running toward us with a slight limp. I shook my head. I knew Nayonni wanted to leave her. I was sure the only reason she didn't was on the strength of me.

Nayonni threw the car in drive and we were on our way. My

mind was all over the place. The one thing I prayed was that we'd be able to get away before any of the men headed back to the house and saw us. She called Corde' back and stayed on the phone with him the entire time that we drove. We ended up meeting him at a gas station that was thirty minutes away from the house and ditched the car we were in.

"Are you okay?" Corde' asked Nayonni. He patted her down and checked her all over to make sure she was good before he came over to check me. He pulled me in for a big bear hug. I could've stayed in his arms forever.

"Did he touch you?" he asked me again. If I didn't answer the first time, it obviously meant that I didn't want to talk about it.

"Can we talk about this later? We have to get out of here. I want a bath and something to eat," I told him. It wasn't that I was trying to be rude. I really was scared and being so close to the house still made me nervous.

"Does anyone have anything on them that can be tracked?" Corde' asked once we were loaded inside of his car.

"This ditzy broad kept her phone," Nayonni told him.

"What the fuck? Naw, you gotta get rid of that, Shawty" Corde' informed her.

"I will, but not this second. Besides, it's not on so he can't track it. Trust me," Mercury commented.

"Trust you? How can we trust you when you wouldn't even help us? You knew I was in that house, tied to a fuckin' chair and not once did you try to help me. How can I trust you at this point?" Nayonni started going off on Mercury. There wasn't anything that Corde' or I could say because her feelings were valid. If the men kept leaving the house and she knew Nayonni was there, she should've tried to work with her so they could've gotten out of there together.

"Give me the phone," Corde' ordered.

"Please. I need to keep it. It has pictures of my daughter. I don't know where she is, and I haven't seen her in a while. Please don't make me get rid of it," Mercury pleaded with him. She was crying loud as hell.

"Don't take her phone," I told Corde'. I know it's probably the right thing to do, but she has a child. It's the only thing she has left of her. If anything, hold on to it and let her get it when it's safe," I softly spoke.

"Are you sure about this, baby?" he asked me. I nodded my head. He stuck his hand out and she hesitantly placed it in his hand.

"Thank you," she said to me.

"Don't thank me yet. I still owe you an ass whooping," I told her.

Sitting in the back with Mercury, I leaned my head back on the seat as Corde' drove away from the gas station. My nerves were on a thousand. I felt as though I was going to have an anxiety attack. I wanted to reach out to my parents, but I couldn't. I didn't want to put their lives in danger. I'd rather them worry about me than to risk reaching out to them and someone going after them to find me. Closing my eyes, I did my best to remain calm. Trying to remain calm caused me to fall asleep. When I woke up, we were pulling into the parking lot of a hotel.

"Where are we?" I asked Corde'.

"We are in Montgomery," he answered me.

"Montgomery, Alabama?" I hollered. "What the hell are we doing here?"

"Think about it, Lyn. They would expect us to go back to New Orleans. We can't go there yet. We have to figure out what's really going on and how to stop them. I need to get y'all in a comfortable bed and fed. I got you, my love," he told me.

After everything that had transpired, I didn't want to trust any man. Since Corde' had never given me a reason not to trust him, I had no choice but to believe him at this point.

"Trust me, babe. I'm not going to hurt you. I'm going to go and get everyone a room and then I'll run get some food."

"Okay, baby. Hurry up. All I want to do is be wrapped in your arms," I admitted to him. Out the corner of my eye, I could see Mercury rolling her eyes and could've sworn I heard her smacking her lips. I didn't say a mumbling word. It was only going to be a matter of time before I had to put her in her place. If she knew what was best for her, she'd leave me the fuck alone.

"Don't be jealous, hoe," Nayonni spat, causing me to giggle. She didn't cut Mercury any slack. "You mad he not giving you any of that BDE?" she asked her.

"BDE? What the fuck is that?" I quizzed, confused as hell. BDE sounded close to an STD and I didn't have time for all that.

"Big Dick Energy, babe. You know how daddy be putting it down," Corde' blurted out, kissing me on the neck and causing me to shiver. There was something about his touch. As much as I was mad at Logic and really wanted to sleep, I was not going to pass up the opportunity to feel Corde' inside of me.

"Whatever. Go get the room, silly," I said.

Corde' got out of the car while we all waited for him. He came back maybe ten minutes later and handed us all a room key. He asked what we wanted to eat and left to go find food. The rooms were close to each other. We knew not to open the room doors unless it was for each other. We had to reiterate the shit to Mercury several times to be sure she understood. She could open the door for somebody that she wasn't supposed to if she wanted. She was going to be on her own.

We were staying at the Renaissance Montgomery Hotel and Spa which was located at the Convention Center. That made me happy. There were a lot of people staying there so it would be hard for anything to happen to us. That's what I kept telling myself to feel comfortable enough to relax. The first thing I did inside the room was take off all of my clothes and get into the shower. I turned the water on until it was steaming hot and allowed it to beat down on my body.

The steam from the shower quickly filled the bathroom. Thankful the shower was walk-in, I sat down at the bottom of it and allowed the water to continue to cover me. It felt good. I wanted to feel safe, but I didn't. I wouldn't feel that way until I knew Logic was out of the way. It was crazy how I was so in love with him a few months back. The love never even left. The way I looked at him changed and therefore, it made it easier for me to not care what happened to him. It would hurt me, but I knew that getting him out of my life was going to be for the best.

## 10

## CORDE'

There was no way for me to describe the way I felt about having Yo-Yo and Lyn back. Mercury, I could've done without. While I went out to get them something to eat, I made it a point to call Kosine. He needed to know that I was coming for their ass.

"Yo?" he answered the phone by the third ring.

"Yo my ass. Fuck you doing, nigga?" I asked.

"I was expecting your call," he stated, chuckling.

"Why the hell you go after my sister and my girl?"

"Your girl? That's my homeboy's wife."

"Cut the shit, Ko! You mad cuz I got what you wanted. That's how you playing? You violated me by going after what was mine," I fumed.

"Going after what was yours? Lyn is married to Logic so she's not yours," he retorted.

"That marriage was a fake. As fake as your ass is. You fucked with my girl and you fucked with my sister. You know it's over for you," I muttered.

"None of that would've happened if you never tried to come after Logic. We ain't do shit to you. You violated and you had to pay for it. I'm going to fuck your sister in every damn hole. Don't worry, I plan on being gentle with her," he announced.

"And how do you plan on doing that?" The fact that he was talking about what he was going to do to my sister led me to believe that he hadn't learned that they were gone yet. At least that's what I thought and I wasn't going to tell him any different. Then again, he could've been playing me to see what I would say. Not wanting to play into any of his games, I continued to act like I didn't know where Lyn and my sister were.

"It doesn't even matter. Just know that I got her."

"If you touch one hair on her head, I'm killing you. You hear me?" I went along with it. If he hadn't learned that she was gone by now, then that bought us a little more time to figure out what we were going to do.

"You ain't going to do shit. Get the fuck off my line, bitch," he chided and hung up on me. I laughed because he didn't know how much trouble he'd gotten himself into. He was a dead man walking.

I grabbed the ladies something from Wendy's so I could get back to the hotel. I didn't put anything past Logic or Kosine's ass. The closer I was to Yo-Yo and Lyn, the better I'd feel. I knocked on Mercury's door and handed her something to eat first.

"All I got was some chili?" she asked me when I handed it to her.

"Naw. I got you some water too," I retorted, handing her a cup of ice water. She rolled her eyes and slammed her door. I didn't give a damn. She was not about to get too comfortable around me knowing how she was with Lyn and my sister. She'd better be glad that her ass got ice in her water. That was me being a little too generous to her ass, if you asked me.

When I got down to Yo-Yo's room, she opened the door laughing. I scratched my head wondering what the fuck she was laughing at. Nobody was supposed to be in there with her and I figured she wasn't crazy enough to make any phone calls.

"What's wrong with you?" I asked her.

"I'm tripping on how you did Mercury," she replied.

"Aye, she got some food, didn't she?" I responded.

"Yeah, but damn? A bowl of chili." She grabbed her stomach and damn near fell forward with laughter.

"It was the large. Damn! Beggars can't be choosy," I quipped.

"I feel ya. Go check on your girl. When she's sleep, come back so we can make some calls and see what we can find out. These niggas got to be handled like yesterday," Yo-Yo voiced.

"You already know I'm with you on that, sis," I told here. I handed her some food and gave her a hug before leaving to go to where Lyn was.

Reaching the room, I patted my pockets in search of the room key. I located it in my back pocket and swiftly pulled it out. I hurried to open the door to check on my girl. She was laid out in the bed naked. The TV was on, but her eyes were closed. It was playing on a low volume. I could hear her softly snoring. I placed her food down and took my clothes off. I went and got in the shower because I hadn't taken a bath since I found out they were missing. It felt good for the water to hit my body. I didn't stay in there long because I wanted to be up under Lyn. Stepping out of the shower, I wrapped a towel around my body and exited the bathroom. When I rounded the corner to where the bed was, Lyn was sitting up, eating.

"I thought you were sleep," I stated when I saw her.

"I was until I smelled the food. Why didn't you wake me up?" she asked me.

"You looked so peaceful. I figured you were tired," I responded.

There was a moment of silence between us as she took a bite out of her burger. She looked so beautiful as she ate. For some reason, I began to visualize us having kids and them sitting around her eating as well. I thought about our daughter looking just like her. It was a beautiful thought. So beautiful that I began to smile.

"What are you smiling for?" she asked. I couldn't tell her the truth, so I made up a lie. I didn't want her to think I was being all weird and shit.

"I'm happy to have you back, baby." Well, it was somewhat a lie. I was happy as hell to have her back.

"Thank you for coming for us."

"You never have to thank me for that. When I told you that I had you, I meant that shit. I'll forever have you. I'll forever come for you. Don't you ever forget that."

"I won't," she stated and leaned in to kiss me.

Lyn handed me my food out the bag. We turned the TV on HBO Max and watched *The Hitman's Wife's Bodyguard.* That was one of my favorite movies. Nobody couldn't tell me that Samuel L. Jackson wasn't a good ass actor because he was the G.O.A.T. I'd argue anybody down about that. Lyn and I laughed and talked throughout the entire movie. She seemed to be at ease which was a good thing. I didn't want her worrying about something I was going to handle. It may not end the way I'm sure she'd like, with Logic alive, but it was going to end, and she'd be able to freely live her life without worrying about looking over her shoulders.

The movie was going off so I went ahead and cleared the bed off. I tossed the covers on top of her before I went to adjust the air on 75 since I didn't like to be in a super cold room. I was about to tell Lyn to get some sleep until she stuck her index finger in the air and wiggled it around, motioning for me to come to her.

"What's up?" I asked, acting like I didn't know what she wanted.

"Come here," she whined and pouted.

"I'm coming. What you need?" I questioned her.

"Baby, come here," she whined again.

"I need for you to get some rest, bae. I thought you were tired."

"I am tired. I need some vitamins to help me go to sleep."

"What you need? Some melatonin?"

"Naw. I need a dose of 'dick me down," she announced, grinning from ear to ear. I couldn't help but laugh. She was smiling, yet I knew her ass was being serious as fuck.

"I got you, girl. Tell me one thing though?"

"What's that?"

"What type of flowers you like?"

"Flowers? Why the fuck are you bringing up flowers when I'm trying to get some dick?"

"I'm asking so I'll know what type of flowers to leave by the bed after I murder that pussy," I joked. We both began laughing. It sounded corny as fuck, yet it put an additional smile on her face. That was the only thing that mattered at that moment.

"No foreplay tonight. All I want is for you to dip inside of me," she announced.

"I gotta get you wet, ma," I told her.

"Get me wet? You being near me makes me wetter than a waterpark. I got this, baby," she stated. She threw the covers off her body to expose her nakedness. I immediately became aroused. I hurried and yanked off the towel that was wrapped around my waist. My dick was already at full attention from the sight of her alone.

Placing my knees on the bed, I crawled toward her. She laid back and opened her legs wide. She was sexy as fuck. I placed a finger between her legs to make sure she was really wet. She wasn't lying. Her pussy was wet-wet. I was nervous I was going to end up busting quick. Lyn must've sensed I was worried. It was either that or I was taking too long to fill her up. She sat up in the bed and grabbed ahold of my dick. She pulled me in closer to her. She leaned back when I was closer to her center. She wasted no time pushing my dick inside of her. She got me halfway there and stopped. I knew it was because she was having to prepare herself for all the dick I was about to give her. I allowed her to lay there with only half of my dick inside of her. I moved it around like I was writing my name in her pussy. After a while, I pushed it the rest of the way in. She let out a loud gasp.

"Corde'," she said my name.

"Yes baby?" I replied.

"I want you inside of me forever," she said. She was talking in the moment. I had to come out of her ass at some point.

"You a trip, girl," I stated, doing my best to play it cool.

"I'm serious, Corde'. I really care about you. I know it's only been a few months but there is something about you that I don't want to lose."

She was opening up to me in the middle of sex. I didn't like that. I've had that happen to me before and it rubbed me the wrong way. From past experiences, people would say anything they thought they had to say in order to keep getting blessed with good dick or pussy. I wasn't that nigga. If she wanted to be open with me, she needed to do it when I wasn't giving her the best dick of her life.

Swiftly, I pulled out of her. I couldn't focus on the task at hand thinking about all the things she'd said to me. I wanted to believe her. At the same time, I questioned if she was saying those things because she was caught up in the moment. Laying down next to her, I tried to think of a respectful way to tell her what was on my mind. She was a woman and with any woman, you have to choose your words carefully. One slip up and they'd be offended by what you said. That was the last thing I needed or wanted.

"What's wrong?" she asked me. "Why'd you stop?"

"How do you know that you really care about me?" I questioned her.

"When I first got with Logic, everything sort of happened so fast. I was so focused on him and what was going on around him that I forgot about what was going on with me. I spent the years that we were together doing the things that I thought would make him happy. He didn't seem to mind. It only made him keep me closer to him," she paused. "At the funeral, I learned that no matter how hard you go for a person or what you do for them, they are going to do what they want to do. He hurt me and it seemed like he didn't give a damn that he did it. He expected me to take what he'd done and act as if it never happened. That was something I couldn't do and certainly wasn't something I was going to tolerate. There were so many times that I had to call him on Kosine being disrespectful to me. He acted like it was no big deal and overlooked the fact that it bothered me. All of those things together made me look at him differently," she paused again. We sat there in silence. It seemed like she was trying to gather her thoughts.

"What's wrong?" I asked, breaking the silence between us.

"I don't want to say the wrong thing," she stated. I sat up in the bed and pulled her closer to me.

"You could never say the wrong thing to me. Tell me what's on your mind. What's in your heart?" I pressed her to open up to me. The way she answered my questions was going to help me determine where we needed to go from here.

"You're different. The way you went off on Mercury and Kazya at the restaurant said a lot. Logic never would've done that shit. You even put Kosine in his place. That was crazy because I'd been asking Logic to do the shit for years and he acted like the way Kosine acted was no big deal. I appreciated you having my back. I felt protected. That was all I ever wanted in a man. I mean, my father did it all my life, but he couldn't give me the love that I could get from a man that I wanted to fully commit and give myself to," she explained.

"Do you think you're over him?" I openly asked. I needed to know. I didn't want to be her rebound. If that's what she was looking for, she was going to have to keep looking. Just like she wanted something worthwhile from me, I expected to receive the same from her.

"I can't lie and say that I don't still have love in my heart for him because I do. I was with that man since I was eighteen.

That's a long time. Especially when he was my first real relationship. The fact that he lied to me, led me to believe that we were married when we really weren't, and he tried to kill me two times is more than enough for me to be done with him for good. A man only has one time to put their hands on me and he's reached his quota with that," she admitted.

"Two times? What do you mean?" Maybe I was being nosey at that point, but I wanted to know what the hell she was talking about.

"The night I thought he had gotten killed, he tried to kill me. We were having sex one minute and the next minute he wrapped his hands around my neck tightly and tried to kill me. He knew about the shit that happened with Kosine. Yet, he never mentioned it to me until that night. It makes me wonder if that was his intentions from the jump. He was going to kill me before he played dead, I guess to eliminate the chance for someone else to be with me. That didn't work out in his favor. When they were holding me at that house, he tried to get Kosine to beat me the way that he'd been beating on Mercury."

"Kosine put his dick beaters on you?"

"No, baby. He refused to do it. That was surprising to me. Kosine has never shown care or concern for anyone as long as I've known him. For him to tell Logic I was a good woman and he'd be a fool to put his hands on me really caught me off guard. However, I can't thank him enough for speaking up for me the way that he did. Imagine if Kosine would've put his hands on me," she remarked, dropping her head.

"If Kosine would've put his hands on you, he would've been somewhere with his eyes permanently shut. This extra air they have to breathe is because I'm allowing it. It's only a matter of time before they both have to go," I admitted to her.

"What do you do?" she asked out of nowhere.

"Excuse me?" I replied. That was my way of avoiding the question.

"Excuse me hell. What type of job do you have where they think you would try to kill Logic?"

"I'm an assassin. That drug shit is not for me. I've lost too many friends and close family members behind drugs so you would never catch me near that shit." That's when I opened up to her about my life as a child and how Yo-Yo put me on. She seemed to be open and understanding of the information I was presenting her with. I was thankful she wasn't judgmental toward me. That was something I probably wouldn't be able to handle.

"Are you prepared to leave that life alone?" she asked out of nowhere.

"That's what I was trying to do. I don't know how the hell we got brought into this shit with Logic and Kosine. When I find out, there is going to be hell to pay. We don't fuck with nobody and don't need people gunning for us. We had one last job to do and that was a month away. That's when I was walking away for good. I'm hoping that Yo-Yo is too. This is only adding to the amount of people we are going to have to body before we can freely walk away," I admitted to her.

"Logic and Kosine?"

"And all the people in their crew who wronged us," I told her. There was no reason for me to lie. She needed to know the truth. These were Logic's last days on earth. If she wanted him, she needed to speak now or forever hold her peace.

"Will you be able to accept that?"

"He's already dead to me," she expressed before sliding down in the bed.

Out of nowhere, Lyn wrapped her short, plump fingers around my dick tightly. There was never a chance for me to object. She quickly devoured my dick. My back lifted off the bed a bit, not being prepared for what she was about to do. Lyn began sucking my dick like she was in a life-or-death situation. She bobbed her head up and down my dick while her hands were focused on my balls. She massaged them like a pro before removing my dick from her mouth. She slid a little further to the foot of the bed and began dipping my balls in and out of her mouth like tea bags. My eyes rolled to the back of my head. Falling back, I placed my arms behind my head and laid there to enjoy everything she was doing to me.

Twisting and turning her hand around my dick, she continued to pleasure my balls. It was too much for me. I gently pushed her back off me. I wanted to be inside of her.

"Come ride your dick, ma," I told her.

Lyn rushed to get in position. Instead of her straddling me and sliding down my dick while she was facing me, she turned and rode my dick in reverse cowgirl position. She was twerking all over my dick. She was basically doing that damn "Buss It" challenge that I'd seen people doing all over *TikTok*.

"Fuck girl. Ride this dick, ma," I loudly stated.

Lyn continued to bounce up and down on my dick. There were a few times when she planted her feet beside me and was practically jumping up and down. She controlled her movement and made sure not to lift up too much so my dick would remain inside of her. Eventually, Lyn did some shit that had me shooting the club up sooner than I wanted to. Without warning, she plopped down on my dick and began slowly grinding. She leaned her body forward to where her head was between my legs. I felt her hand touching my feet. I thought she was gripping them to maintain balance while being on top of me until I felt something moist on my big toe. Lyn's crazy ass had put my fuckin' foot in her mouth and was suckin' on my damn toes while she was still grinding on my dick.

"What the fuckkkkkkk!!" I grunted.

Whatever she was doing to me felt good as fuck. I couldn't hold my nut in any longer. Lyn must've sensed it. She grinded faster and sucked my toe harder.

"Damnit Lyn. I can't take this shit!"

For some reason, my body started shaking. That was the shit

her body normally did when she was on the verge of climax. My damn soul must've left my body at that point.

"Let that shit go, Corde'. Give me my vitamins, baby," Lyn seductively spoke before jumping off me. She replaced her pussy with her mouth. As soon as I felt it tightly wrap around my dick, it was over. There was no way I could hold it in any longer. My nut freely flowed from my dick, coating her throat. Lyn took it all in and swallowed it on some pornstar type shit. She had the nerve to look me in the eye, open her mouth so I could see that she swallowed it, and then licked her fuckin' lips. The only thing I could do at that point was lay there. She'd fucked me up mentally with that shit.

"You okay, baby?" she asked, breaking the silence that had been between us for the past few minutes.

"Mmmm hmmm..." I replied, my eyes were still closed. I needed a minute to find my soul again.

"Good. Wake my dick up. I'm not done with him yet," she ordered. My eyes bucked. Lyn had me fucked up. She had sucked all of the energy out of me. I was good for bouncing back quick and being ready to get back in the pussy, but not this time. She drained me. She knew what the fuck she'd done.

"You gotta wait, baby. I'm not ready yet," I sadly admitted.

"Whattttt?!? You mean to tell me that you tapping out after the first round? Damnnnn..." she joked. She was poppin' big shit. I knew I was going to have to shut her up. There was no way I was going to let her punk me.

"Fuck all that. You want some more of this dick? Huh?" I asked. Her eyes grew the size of golf balls. She wasn't prepared for what I was about to do next.

Flipping her over on her stomach, I climbed on her back and quickly pushed inside of her.

"Too deepppppp..." she whined.

"Naw. You talked all that shit. Take this mufuckin' big ass dick," I demanded, pushing deeper inside of her. I delivered stroke after stroke to her. They were long, deep, and satisfying.

She was flat down on her stomach with my body pressed against her back.

"How that shit feel, ma?"

"It feels sooooo good. Keep fuckin' me just like that," she begged me to continue to pleasure her. I smiled as I pressed further down inside of her and started rotating my hips. I grinded inside of her the way she'd grinded on my dick not even ten minutes earlier.

"Sssss...." she hissed.

"Mmmm hmmmm...Talk all that shit you were talking a minute ago. You wanna give a nigga outer body experiences and shit and think you not 'bout to get your wig fucked off your head," I mentioned. She wasn't really wearing a wig. She had a sew-in in her head. From the way I was fuckin' her, I wouldn't be surprised if I was able to knock the thread loose on her shit and it was barely hanging on by the time I got done.

"Fuck me, Cordde'. I've been a bad girl. Punish your pussy, baby," she requested.

"Say no more," I replied, obliging her every request.

Dipping in and out of her, I was loving everything transpiring between us. I placed my palms down next to her and was basically doing push-ups on her. My dick glided in and out of her. Each time I went down, I pushed a little deeper inside of her and did a grinding motion. Lyn's moans became louder and louder. She continuously begged for me to fuck her until she claimed she couldn't take it anymore. She came three times before I was finally at a point of busting again myself.

My body dropped to the side of her when I was done. If I wasn't done the first time, I was completely out of energy that time. I'd given Lyn everything that I had. Hopefully, it was enough to show her that when it came down to sex, she'd never have the upper hand. When we were finished, I got a warm, soapy towel and cleaned us both up. Placing the towel on the night stand, I got back in the bed with her and pulled her close to me.

"Thank you," she said out of nowhere.

"Huh? What are you thanking me for?" I curiously asked.

"You haven't said it yet, but I feel it. I don't know where things are going with us, but I love it. I'm glad you're in my life. I'm thanking you in advance for the way you're going to love me," she voiced before placing her head on my chest. No other words were spoken between us as we both closed our eyes.

# 11

# LOGIC

"What you find?" I called Kosine to see if he'd found out anything. We'd been gone away from the house the entire day. I needed to get back to Lyn. I wasn't done punishing her for her betrayal.

"I ain't found shit. What about you?" he told me.

"Nothing. We need to find out how the hell Yo-Yo's ass got away," I replied.

"She got away because she outsmarted Witt's dumb ass. We need to hire better workers," he fussed.

"Yeah. You're right. We need to head back to the house and check on the girls. Have you heard from Butta and them?" Butta was one of the men we left at the house to look after the women.

"No. I haven't heard from nobody," he paused. "I did get a call from Day-Day's ass. He knows we took his sister."

"What did he say?"

"Something about if we touch a hair on her head, he was going to kill us."

"He knows that she got away. He wouldn't have called you if he thought we still had her. That nigga would've rolled up on us. Since she's gone, she knows where we are. That's why them clowns came out there shooting at us. We need to get the girls and get the hell out of dodge."

"Why are we running? You scared?" he asked me.

"Scared? Nigga, I ain't never scared. At the same time, I don't need a mufucka pulling up on me when I'm trying to get to the bottom of shit. If you want to stay there, that's on you. I'm about to get my bitch and bounce," I told him.

"You need to use her as bait," Kosine suggested.

"Bait for what?"

"For Day-Day. You know he wants her. That nigga will come after her if he thinks he can save her. We can use Lyn as a way to get him on our turf and kill his monkey ass."

Although I didn't want to put Lyn out there like that, Kosine made a lot of sense. If Day-Day was checking for Lyn the way that Kosine said he was, he should have no problem trying to come save her.

"Aight. Let's meet back up at the house and we can get the shit set up."

"Bet," he said, and we ended the call.

Happy moments with Lyn crossed my mind. She wasn't a disloyal woman so everything that was happening was throwing me off. I was mad at her for stepping out on me with Day-Day, but it really wasn't her fault. She did the same thing any other woman would've done. As a matter of fact, the more I thought about it, the more I realized that I was the reason she even ended up in his arms. I heard how she was when she thought I was dead. If the shit at the funeral never happened and she didn't learn about Kazya's bitch ass, Lyn would've still been mourning me. She would've been happy to see a nigga when I popped back into her life. That made me call Kazya. I wanted to know what made her and my mother think it was okay for her to go to the funeral and reveal everything the way that they did.

Gathering my thoughts, I picked the phone up and called Kazya. The phone rang a few times before going to voicemail. I waited about five minutes to see if she was going to call me back.

It wasn't like her to not answer. If she didn't answer, she would quickly call me back. After those five minutes passed and I didn't get an answer, I called my mother's phone. She answered by the second ring

"Yes Logic?" she said when she answered.

"Hey to your ass too," I stated.

"Don't tell me how to answer my fuckin' phone. What do you want? Sent those damn people to my house threatening me and shit," she spat.

"What? What people?" I was confused as hell about what she was talking about. "Maw, what are you talking about?"

"Some men came to my house earlier today. They told me that if I opened my mouth to say anything, they were going to kill me."

She was rambling but I didn't understand what the rambling was about. Why the hell would she think I would send someone to her house and why the hell would she think I would tell them to tell her to keep anything from me? For her to even say that sounded stupid as fuck.

"Maw, what the fuck are you talking about? Listen to yourself. Why the hell would I send someone to threaten you? I've never had a problem telling you anything that I wanted you to know whether it was good or bad. What are you talking about?" She suddenly got quiet. I wasn't sure what the hell was going on, but I didn't like it.

"I gotta go, son. My medicine just got here," she told me. That was her code for telling me her dealer was there. She was about to get high off some crack and I wasn't going to hear from her ass for a week or so. I couldn't let her get off the phone without her telling me either what was going on or where the hell Kazya's ugly ass was.

"Hold on, maw. Tell me where Kazya is before you hang up."

"I don't know. She came by here last week and left those ugly ass babies here. I ain't seen or heard from her since. The bitch not even answering my calls."

"I know you aren't watching the kids out the goodness of your heart. What's the catch?'

"She's been sending somebody by here every two days to supply me with my medicine so I ain't been complaining."

"Maw, who's been coming by there? Kazya wouldn't even have the money to pay for no shit like that."

"I thought the same thing. The medicine I'm getting these days are a high grade. She gotta be paying a hell of a lot for it. I thought maybe you had something to do with it. Especially when one of your lil' friends came by here," she commented.

"One of my friends. Who maw? Who are you talking about?"

***Spiff... Spiff...***

Out of nowhere, I heard a familiar sound. It was the sound of a gun going off that had a silencer attached to it. The only reason I heard it so well was because she was on the phone when she was hit. Someone had killed her to keep her quiet, but who? Why?

Not a single tear fell from my eyes as I hung the phone up. I continued on toward the house we'd been hiding out at. Whomever went after my mother was someone that I knew. Someone that she knew. My judgement was clouded. I didn't know who to trust at this point. By the time I made it back to the house, there were police cars lined up everywhere. I stopped at the end of the road and made a U-turn. I'd be dumb trying to go down the road to figure out what was going on. I hit Kosine back on his phone. At first, he didn't answer. He called me back damn near twenty minutes later. When I asked why he didn't answer, he said it was because he was on the phone trying to find out what was going on. He was stuttering and shit. He was hiding something.

"I'm about to send you an address. It's not far from where we were staying. Get there fast," he instructed me. I didn't like the way he was talking or how he sounded. It was a sign that something bad had happened and something else was potentially about to pop off.

Kosine was right about the new location being near the old one. Twenty minutes later and I was pulling into the driveway. It seemed like another damn trap house. I wasn't about to stay at another one. It was fine when we were holding Yo-Yo hostage. Since she'd gotten away, it was no reason for us to continue to live like that. I pulled into the driveway and shut the car off. Hopping out the car, I marched toward the front door. Kosine came out and met me in the yard.

"What the hell is going on?" I asked when we were in close proximity of each other.

"The girls are gone," he roared.

"What the hell you mean? Where the fuck is Butta and Buck?" I questioned, not understanding how the hell they could've gotten away when we had someone there watching them.

"Them niggas dead," he grunted.

"How the hell you know?" I was still confused on what the fuck was going. Everything seemed to be falling apart and I didn't like that shit. I was losing control and that was not like me. I was never someone that moved in a sloppy manner. Somebody had to be sabotaging me and what the fuck I had going on. It had to be someone on the inside of my organization. As bad as I didn't want to believe Kosine would be behind it, all signs pointed to his ass.

"I sent Damon back to the house when I couldn't get Butta and them on the phone. He called me and told me that the girls were gone, and someone had killed those niggas. I told him to set the place on fire, but he couldn't. He heard sirens nearing so he had to get the hell away from there. That's when I had him to go out and find somewhere else for us to meet. I couldn't call and tell you what the hell was going on because you know we don't discuss that kind of shit on the phone," he explained.

"Day-Day has to die!" I barked. I meant that shit. He was causing me more trouble than he was worth.

"I agree with you."

***Ding...***

My phone went off with a notification from Facebook. It said that I had a friend request. The timing of it was crazy. I glanced at the phone and was about to put it back in my pocket until I looked at it again.

"What the fuck!" I muttered as I opened the little blue app on my phone.

"What is it?" Kosine asked me.

"Why you send me a fuckin' friend request on Facebook, nigga? Why the hell are you even on Facebook at this time? We got too much shit going on for you to be on social media," I fussed.

"What the fuck are you talking about? I'm standing right here. You don't see me with a phone in my hand," he retorted.

"Maybe you sent it earlier and it's a delayed notification. You know we out in the boonies. The damn phone probably just got a good enough signal to send me the notification."

"Why the hell would I send you a friend request when we are already friends? You are out of your mind right now," he bellowed. That was something for me to question. Even though we were barely on social media, we used it when we needed to find out something about someone. It was a way for us to keep up with what was going on around us and it made us not look so suspect. How many thug ass niggas do you know spend time on social media? Exactly.

From first glance, I thought it was Kosine that sent the request because it was his name. I clicked on the profile and became angry as hell. Then I started laughing.

"Aye, somebody gunning for your ass," I told him, still laughing.

"What the hell is so funny?" he asked.

"Somebody sending out friend requests with your name on it. You won't believe what they are using for the profile picture," I stated.

"What?" he queried, reaching for my phone.

"A picture of your lil' ass dick," I hollered.

Kosine's phone went off at that time. He must've gotten the same request.

"My dick not lil'. What the hell makes you think that's my dick?" he asked, staring at his phone and pulling up the page.

"It's the same tattoo you got on your stomach," I acknowledged, pointing at his stomach.

The person behind the page was someone that had to have been close to Kosine. They were able to get pictures of him while he was naked. That meant it was a bitch. That shit was funny as hell. When Mercury kept telling Lyn that Kosine's dick was small, I thought she was being like a typical woman. When they get mad, they say all kinds of bullshit about you. Yet, she was not lying this time. That nigga shit was smaller than my mufuckin' pinky. I don't know who did the shit but when Kosine got his hands on them, it was going to be trouble.

"That ain't my dick. That shit photoshopped," he grunted before punching the side of my car.

"Aye, calm the fuck down. Don't be hitting my shit. It ain't my fault somebody fuckin' with you," I muttered.

"Ain't nobody behind that shit but Mercury's bitch ass. I'm going to kill her," he ranted. As he continued to go off, I noticed that his phone was ringing. He kept hitting the button on the side of his phone to send it to voicemail. That made me even more suspicious of him. There was no reason for him to be declining a call unless he was trying to keep something from me.

"You should've killed her a long time ago," I voiced. The way he was always beating her, it was shocking she was still breathing.

"I kept her around because she was trained. I don't have time to train anyone else the way I had her trained."

"Seems to me like you're going to be starting over again anyways. She got away. That bitch not coming back." I couldn't help but laugh. The expression on his face didn't make things any better. It only caused me to laugh harder.

"Fuck you! Lyn not coming back either," he grunted.

"Don't worry about my bitch. Worry about what the fuck you got going on," I fussed.

"Yeah. You don't like when people talking reckless to you about your property, huh? How the hell you think I feel? I told you that you were going to respect me, and I meant that shit," he fumed.

"Whatever. Mind the business that pays you. Lyn is coming back. Watch what I tell you." The words sounded good leaving my mouth, but I didn't believe them. Truth was, I was scared. For the first time in my life, I was really scared.

Lyn was everything to me. That's why I fought so hard to keep her around. Even though our marriage was a sham, she should've appreciated the fact that I went through so much trouble to pretend to be married so I could make her happy. What woman wouldn't love that? She was ungrateful. Yeah! That bitch wanted somebody to move heaven and earth for her. It doesn't work like that. Life doesn't work like that. My mind was all over the place. There was no way for me to think straight.

"What's the plan?" Kosine asked.

"What you mean?" I replied.

"I mean what the hell are we going to do now?"

"I'll figure something out. I need to go clear my head."

Leaving Kosine standing outside, I headed back to my car. Jumping inside, I darted away from him. Finding out who was after me should've been my number one priority, but it wasn't. I was more concerned with getting to Lyn. If anybody wanted me dead, this would be the perfect time to make it happen. My mind was only on Lyn, so I wasn't thinking straight. I wasn't the same logical person I was known for being. All of this was Lyn's fault. She was going to be the death of me.

## 12

# MERCURY

*THE NEXT DAY*

Lyn and Nayonni seemed to be on some bonding type of shit. I couldn't lie and say that I wasn't jealous because I was. I'd always longed for friends and never had them. That was because Kosine kept me away from everyone. I had a chance to build something with Lyn, but I allowed my jealousy to stop that. They had some type of connection and I didn't understand what it was. They freely spoke with each other and cracked jokes in an attempt to make light of the situation. The whole time, I was a nervous wreck. I hadn't seen or spoken with my daughter. When I asked Kosine where she was, he said that she was with his mother. I didn't understand that because he never visited his mother or anyone else in his family. Nobody other than Logic.

Day-Day made us get up early to go shopping. We needed some clothes and he said he had a few errands to run. He allowed us to take the car while he stayed back at the hotel. I took it that since we were nowhere near Kosine and Logic and since Yo-Yo was with us, he felt safe letting us go out on our own.

"When are we supposed to be going back to New Orleans?" I asked, breaking up the fit of laughter Yo-Yo and Lyn were in. Yo-Yo had said something, and Lyn ate the shit up. She was laughing so hard you would've thought Yo-Yo should've been on the stage of *Deaf Comedy Jam* or something.

"Why? You got somewhere to be?" Yo-Yo quizzed.

"I want to find my daughter," I admitted to her. Yo-Yo got quiet.

"When was the last time you saw her?" Lyn finally spoke up.

"It's been so long that I can't remember. All I know is that I'm worried about her and I miss her. I want Kosine to pay for all of this shit." For some reason, I began to cry. All I wanted was my daughter and people seemed to not understand that.

"We'll get her back," Lyn said something to comfort me. It made me feel better to hear but I was scared that she was only saying it to get me to calm down.

"We not about to do all that crying and shit. If she's alive, we'll find her and get her back," Yo-Yo chimed in. "Mercury, I'm going to be honest with you. I don't like you. I don't want to do anything to help you. If we find out your daughter is alive, we will help you get her back simply because she's innocent. If she's not, I can't guarantee that we are going to do anything to help you get revenge. You will be on your own with that," she asserted. I couldn't be mad at her.

"Thank you."

"Don't thank me just yet. Go ahead and tell me everything that happened the last time you saw her," Yo-Yo advised me.

"Let me show you a picture of her first," I said. Something told me that if she saw how precious Jovi was, she'd be more sympathetic about the situation.

Yo-Yo didn't get a chance to respond. Opening up the center console of the car where Day-Day had placed my phone, I pulled it out and turned it on.

"What the hell are you doing? They can track your phone," Yo-Yo yelled.

"It's not going to be on long. I'm sure his ass not up at this time trying to track me," I commented. Even though the words came out of my mouth, I didn't believe the shit myself.

"It only takes seconds for him to go into the find my iPhone app and ping your location. What are you thinking?" Lyn asked.

"Watch..." I replied. The phone powered on and I immediately went to the settings and turned off the location as well as the ability to find the phone. If he was going to track the phone, it was going to ping to my last location which was with him.

Lyn and Yo-Yo stared at me with confusion. They didn't say anything. Satisfied that my phone couldn't be tracked, I went straight to my pictures. I pulled up all types of pictures of Jovi and showed them to Lyn and Yo-Yo. Lyn had seen her before but that didn't stop her from admiring my baby. The more I scrolled through the pictures, I noticed random photos popping up. Out of nowhere, a picture that I'd taken of Kosine while he was sleeping popped up. I swiftly swiped to the right to see the number of photos I had of him. That was when I got an idea on how to start getting back at his ass. He was not going to easily get away with what he had done to me.

"I'm going to get his ass," I told Lyn and Yo-Yo who were still silent. "Look at this shit. For years, I allowed him to push his snail sized dick inside of me for nothing. He had the nerve to think he got me pregnant. I had a better chance of getting pregnant by my damn thumb," I snapped. I rambled on and on about the pain I'd endured from him.

"You let a nigga with a dick like that beat on you? Damn, bitch. What you get out of the deal?" Yo-Yo joked and Lyn laughed. I cracked a small smile even though I truly felt dumb. She had me thinking about what I really got out of being with Kosine and the truth was, I got absolutely nothing out of being with him. Nothing but my ass beat day in and day out.

"Shut up, Yo-Yo. She loved him. She was like me and thought that he'd be able to change her life and he only made things worse. At first, things seem perfect but as you go on, you find out more and more about the demon you're lying down with. That's why I'm scared to start over with Corde'," Lyn honestly spoke.

"You can get that out of your head. My brother ain't shit like Logic or Kosine. You see how selective he has been with women? He could've had any woman he wanted, but he wanted the right woman. He was waiting for you. If you hurt my brother, know that I'm going to beat your ass," she threatened Lyn. Lyn's smile turned into a frown. Yo-Yo's face remained serious the entire time. For the first time, I felt a hint of tension between them. It felt weird, yet good at the same time. I hated always feeling like the person that was despised in the group.

"I'm not going to hurt him. The only way I'll hurt him is if he hurts me and I have to fuck him up. Understand?" Lyn remarked. Her facial expression was now as serious as Yo-Yo's. It was then that I realized I needed to change the subject. If I didn't, them hoes were probably going to engage in a shoot-out to see who had the biggest balls out of the two and I didn't have time for that.

"What's the name of a gay dating site?" I asked out of nowhere.

"What you mean?" It took some time, but Yo-Yo finally turned to answer me.

"What are the dating sites that gay men use?" I inquired again.

"Do we look gay to you? How the hell should we know?" Yo-Yo snapped. If there was ever a woman that I'd never seen with a soft spot, it was her ass. She had to have an attitude about everything. Maybe it was due to the question coming from me. Damn. She needed to cut me some slack. I fucked up by not helping and I realized that. She didn't need to keep trying to penalize me for the shit.

"Hold on. Let me see your phone, Yo-Yo," Lyn said and held her hand out to receive the phone. Although hesitant, Yo-Yo handed the phone right over to her.

"Hey Siri?"

"Good afternoon. How can I help?" Siri replied.

"Hey Siri, what are some gay dating sites?" Lyn stated into the phone. Siri came back with a list of at least seven sites. The only one I recognized off the list was the site called Grindr.

"Wait! Why do you want to know about gay dating sites?" Yo-Yo quizzed.

"I'm about to create lover boy a profile. Maybe somebody will roll up on his ass. Matter fact, I'm going to find a few men and say he's interested in a rough gangbang," I advised them. I laughed thinking about a group of men showing up to give him the best dick of his life.

"Bruhhhhh... You ain't shit, but I'm here for it. Let me help you create the profile," Yo-Yo asserted. She took the phone out of my hand and started completing the profile.

"I think his dick pick should be his profile picture," Yo-Yo suggested.

"No. That's going to make them flag the account," I commented.

"You're right. Let's find a full body picture of him where he's dressed up and his muscles popping out and shit."

"Y'all, I'm all for the fun and games. But this is not the right way to do this. You're going to get some innocent people killed," Lyn finally spoke up.

"What you mean? How would we get them killed?"

"You are about to create a profile for this straight, crazy man, on a gay website. Kosine not an ugly dude so you know these niggas are going to bite at that shit. If they try to pull up on him for real, he is going to kill them. Don't play dumb. Don't put these men in harm's way if you don't have to," Lyn seethed.

"Fine. We'll put his phone number in the bio part and allow the men to reach out to him before meeting him. That way he'll have a chance to cuss them out instead of killing them," Yo-Yo said.

"Sounds good to me," I returned. Yo-Yo went to work

completing the profile. When she was done, she showed it to Lyn and me. There was no denying her ass was good. She knew exactly what to put in the profile to grab people's attention. If I were a man, I'd be one of the first people to go for him. Like Lyn said, Kosine was far from ugly. That man was so fine, it had me overlooking the dumb shit he did for years.

"How does this sound?" Yo-Yo asked us. She passed the phone around to show us what she'd written under the bio information for Kosine's profile.

***"Strong black man living in the 504. Looking for a man to complete me 702. First, I'd like to a little fun. Gangbangs with big cocks are my dream 3702. Put my number together and hit me up."***

"Who the hell says cocks?"

"Kosine's ass does today. Ain't nobody gonna know."

"You a lie. Look at him. Does he look like the type of man that would let the word cock roll off his tongue?"

"Fine. I'll change it to big Ds. I thought it was funny though."

"I can't believe you put his actual number up there. You think people are going to go for it?"

"Yelp. Let me add a few more pictures, including the one of his baby carrot and we'll see what happens."

Yo-Yo did everything she wanted to do and handed me the phone back. That's when I took it upon myself to create a Facebook and Instagram account for him. That gay dating profile was hit or miss. I needed to put something out there that I knew people would surely see. Once I created his profile on those two sites, I sent a friend request to all the people I knew he knew. I made sure to send him one too so he'd know someone was fuckin' with him. I'm sure he was going to put two and two together and see that it was me behind all of this. I didn't care. I had no plans of being close to him again, so there was really nothing he could do to me at this point.

"Let's go shopping ladies," Yo-Yo emphasized. She threw the car in drive and we were well on our way.

Messing with Kosine at this point was either going to be the best or worse decision of my life. Yet, I felt like there was really nothing for me to lose. I'd made up in my mind that I was going to make sure he got everything he deserved. Whether it came from me or someone else... Kosine was going to have to pay me for my tears.

# 13

## KOSINE

For whatever reason, my phone kept going off. I was getting text and calls from numbers I didn't know. With Logic away, it gave me the time I needed to bust a few moves on my own without worrying about getting caught. Paying Chico a visit was the first thing I decided to do. He'd been blowing my phone up. I knew it wasn't because he went to handle the business I asked him to handle. It was because I had something he wanted. The only way for him to get them back was to do what he was paid to do.

"Yeah?" I stated into the phone when I answered.

"Yo, somebody came into my crib and took my family," he whined. I wanted to laugh because he was sounding like a true bitch.

"What? Where are you?" I did my best to act like I cared.

"I'm at home," he told me.

Chico didn't stay far from where I was. He kept his family up in an apartment in Etheridge for whatever reason. He must've thought nobody would catch on to the shit because he did make a little money in the streets. He was wrong. I knew everything that I needed to know about the people that I dealt with. Nobody was exempt from me knowing their business. I told him

I was headed his way and hung the phone up on him. Like I said, he didn't live far from where I was.

My gas light popped on when I was enroute to my destination. I had to pull over to the nearest gas station. There was no way I was going to risk running out of gas. I'd never been the type of nigga that walked anywhere. That wasn't about to start today.

Pulling up to the first pump, I noticed a chick standing on the opposite side putting gas in her whip. I quickly got out of my ride and walked over to where she was.

"You need some help, ma?" I asked her.

"I got it," she replied.

"Let me do it for you. You're too fine to be out here having to put gas in your own car."

"You gonna pay for the gas too?" she asked me and winked.

"Hell yeah, I'll pay for it." She was driving a little ass Honda Civic. I knew it wouldn't cost much to fill her up. She must've been down on her luck to even ask for me to pay for the gas. She'd just met me and didn't even know my name. The fact that she felt so comfortable even suggesting the idea to me let me know that she had done the shit before. She was probably a pro at getting men to do whatever she wanted them to do.

"Okay. Thank you," she stated and ran her right index finger seductively down my chest while she sucked on her left index finger. It was sexy until I glanced at her mouth and noticed she had braces. I didn't knock people who wore braces because it actually made some people look ten times better than what they originally looked. That wasn't happening in her case. She had more gaps in her mouth than a jack-o-lantern and she had all of these dark spots throughout her mouth. That was clearly where she had to have cavities filled. That wasn't cute. It sure as hell wasn't sexy. Ole girl didn't take care of her teeth so I knew she couldn't do shit for me.

"What are you waiting on and why are you staring at me like that?" she asked and winked at me again.

"I realized I had to do something. I'm going to have to pass right now."

"Pass for what? I'll make it worth your while," she informed me.

"Naw, I'm good, ma. You have a good day. I need to handle something." People always said that I was cruel. Not this time. I was being nice as hell. Yet, she was pushing the other side of me to come out by continuously questioning me after I already told her that I was good.

"Fuck you then. Bum ass nigga. I can get my own gas," she spat and pranced toward the inside of the store. Not feeling the way she'd spoke to me; I followed her right inside the store. If I had to beat her ass in there, I had no problem doing so. I didn't give a damn who you were, you were going to respect me. All she had to do was leave well enough alone and walk away. She couldn't, she had to get in the last word. That was when she fucked up.

She trampled right on inside the store and walked right up to the register.

"Can I get five on pump three?" she asked the cashier.

"Oh, I get it. You were tripping because you didn't have any money," I mentioned.

"Don't tell me what I have. You don't know me," she barked.

"I ain't got to know you to see that all you could afford to ask for was five funky ass dollars. Here with your dusty ass," I stated and pulled a wad of cash out of my pocket. I began peeling off one-dollar bills and tossing them at her ass. As I suspected, the bitch had the nerve to bend over and begin picking them up.

"Stripper ass bitch," I shouted at her.

She brushed up against me a few times while she was picking the money up. That immediately made me want to go wash my hands.

"Aye, where the toilet?" I rudely asked the cashier. She pointed toward an area in the right corner of the store. Not one time did she look up to acknowledge me.

"Rude bitch," I spat and marched in the direction of the bathroom. Placing my hand inside my shirt, I put it on the door and yanked it open. I typically didn't use public restrooms, but this was an emergency. I didn't know where the hell shorty had been, especially with her seeming homeless and shit.

It seemed like the minute I hit the bathroom my bladder started fuckin' with me. A weird urge to pee came upon me. Luckily, there were urinals lined up against the wall. All I had to do was pull my mans out and go to work. No sooner than I unzipped my pants and pulled my dick out did the bathroom door fly open. With the line of business I was in, I was on high alert. It didn't help that Day-Day and Yo-Yo were gunning for Logic and me.

"Aye, you need to wait until I le-" I turned to say but my words were halted by the chick immediately dropping down to her knees and putting my dick in her mouth. I thought about debating since I'd seen how corroded her mouth was. Yet, it felt good and I hadn't been around Mercury to get my dick sucked so I decided to let her finish.

"Hol' up," I stated. "Hol' your mouth open for me, ma," I told her and backed away. Still on her knees, she kept her mouth wide open. With good aim, the pee I was holding in came shooting out and into her mouth. I loved that kinky shit and apparently, she did too because she didn't move at all.

When I was done, she closed her mouth and allowed the pee to run out the sides of it. I wasn't sure if she thought that was sexy, but it wasn't. It actually pissed me off because she was supposed to swallow the shit.

"The fuck is you doing?" I questioned her. She stayed kneeled before me with a big ass ugly grin on her face.

"What you mean? You told me to stay down here and I did. I caught your pee in my mouth," she commented.

"You were supposed to swallow it," I grunted.

"Swallow it? I don't swallow shit. Not unless the price is right. If you paying then I'll do whatever you want. Hell, you can fuck me in the ear as small as your dick is." She giggled. That enraged me. Without warning, I lifted my foot and kicked her in the face. Both teeth and blood shot out of her mouth as she fell back to the floor.

"If you tell anybody about this, I'm coming back to kill your ass," I spat right as I bent down to take her purse. Grabbing her driver's license out, I showed it to her and then placed it in my pocket. That was my way of letting her know that I'd be able to find her, so she needed to be on her best behavior.

Poking my head out of the bathroom, I observed the area to see if anyone was watching. It wasn't a busy gas station, so I was able to slide out of the door without anyone noticing me. I tossed forty-five dollars on the counter for my gas and exited the gas station. After getting my gas, I continued my journey to Chico.

By the time I pulled up on Chico, it was starting to get dark. That worked in my favor in the event he said the wrong thing and I had to go ahead and kill him. There was no way I was going to leave him alive if he was going to be a threat to me. By threat, I meant him having the potential to rat me out and try to get out of dodge.

***Knock... Knock...***

Showing him some type of courtesy, I knocked on his door and allowed him the chance to answer. He came to the door disheveled. He was a nervous wreck. His clothes were hanging off him and his hair was all over his head. Entering the house, I shut and locked the door behind me. Refocusing my attention on Chico, I noticed him constantly pacing back and forth.

"Here," I said to him before going into my pocket. I walked over to the fireplace mantle with my stash in my hand that I'd removed from my pocket. Pouring it on the fireplace, I pulled out everything I was going to need so we could snort. It was all we both needed to calm down.

"I don't want that shit. You don't need it either. That's why your ass is so mufuckin' crazy," he stated. He started going off and saying all kinds of shit to me that was uncalled for. It angered me more than he could imagine.

While Chico continued to talk shit, I went to work getting my fix. I gave it some time to get into my system and give me the high I wanted before I chose to handle him. When he least expected it, I grabbed Chico by the back of the neck and proceeded to beat his head against the fireplace. For some reason, images of Mercury and Lyn flashed in my head. Mercury had to be handled. She knew that leaving me was never an option and she did it anyway. Lyn was going to get what was coming to her too. She was fighting against me too much. She knew that I wanted her, and she was turning me down. Nobody turned me down. She was going to be mine. I was determined to make that happen.

"Please. Stoooopppp!" Chico cried, begging me to let him go. His cries were the only thing that knocked me out of my trance. Since he lived in an apartment, there was a chance someone could hear him. I didn't need the added attention. The last time somebody got in my business, they ended up losing their life. I'd hate for it to happen to someone else.

"You a bitch!" I barked at Chico before slinging him across his sofa. He landed on the floor. I marched around to the back of the couch and was preparing to pick him up. He was on his knees crawling to get away from me. Reaching down, I picked him up by the neck and pressed him up against the wall.

"Come on, Ko! I'll do whatever you want. Why are you doing this?"

"You're damn right you're going to do everything I tell you. I'm in charge. Not Logic! I am, nigga. If I tell you to jump off a mufuckin' bridge, you'd damn sure better do it," I roared. "You will kill Logic like I said or you're never going to see your family again."

"You have my family? You did this shit?" He must've thought about it. Chico developed a new strain of energy and began bucking like a horse.

"Calm your mufuckin' ass down or you'll never see them again. I'm not playing with you. All I have to do is make one phone call and it's over for them," I assured him. It took some time, but he tired himself out. That was enough for me to slam him up against the wall and watch him drop like a fly. "Next time do what the fuck I said. You have two weeks to handle this shit. I'm done playing with you."

Chico laid on the floor damn near lifeless. The fact that he was still breathing gave me reason not to worry. Whether I said what I said in a nice or hood way, that nigga heard what the fuck I said. If he knew what was good for him, his ass was going to take heed to my warning and do what he was paid to do.

# 14
# LOGIC

Kosine thought his ass was slick. No matter how much he tried to hide what he was up to, I made it a point to be two steps ahead of him. As soon as I drove out of the yard and left Kosine standing there looking dumbfounded, something felt wrong. He was up to something and I wanted to know what it was. He was upset about someone creating the Facebook profile and pretending to be him. There was no way anybody could've blamed him. Did I believe Mercury was behind the shit? It was hard not to believe it. He'd done more than enough damage to her for her to come after him. She wanted revenge and what better way to get it than by humiliating him?

From the time Kosine got in the car, stopped at the gas station, and went inside some man's apartment, I'd kept eyes on him. The whole time, I wondered what he was doing. Every move he made; he was strategic in doing so. I laughed when I saw him talking to Judy. She was the neighborhood crackhead. It was only a matter of time before he realized that. When he did, he immediately shot her down, and her reaction was priceless. None of that bothered me. I knew his temper and knew that he would snap at any moment without warning. What made me curious about everything he'd done was when he paid the mysterious man a visit. We told each other everything. Why didn't he tell me where he was going or what he was going there for? It had me wondering if there was some truth behind the Facebook profile. Was he going to see a man for personal pleasure and didn't want me to know? He was in there long enough to get a nut in.

"You good?" I asked him when he came out of the apartment and made it back to his car.

"What the fuck are you doing here? So, you following me now?" Kosine hollered.

"Again... You good nigga? You doing all that sweating and shit. What you had to do over here?"

"Why are you questioning me? You are not my daddy, nigga," Kosine blurted out. He moved away from his car and started walking toward mine. That's when I stepped out of the car. He inched up on me and got in my face.

"I'd suggest you pump your brakes. I'm not one of these average ass niggas. You're going to fuck around and get yourself killed fuckin' with me," I honestly told him.

Things between Kosine and I were strained. That was due to him acting as if he didn't know his place. When I hit these streets, he was in jail. I told him I was going to hook him up when I started doing good which was going to be around the time he got out. I had that much faith in myself. At first proposition, he turned me down. He said some shit about wanting to stay clean to avoid going back to jail. That was understandable.

However, when I started making this bread and he saw it, he wanted in. I told him he could work with me. It was a partnership, but he was more of a silent partner. I'd always been the one making all of the decisions and making sure everything ran smoothly. He was okay with it at first. That was until he wanted to run in on people and take their territories. I told him that wasn't the way to go. It wasn't logical and I was not about to put myself in a position where the cops were going to start eyeballing everything I did.

"I'm sick of your shit, Logic. You coming at me sideways when you need to be going after Day-Day and Yo-Yo. They are the ones who came after you. They are killing the people you love left and right. You see what happened to your mother." As soon as he said that alerts went off in my head. Who told him what happened to my mother? I hadn't told a soul and it just happened, so you know it wasn't on the news yet.

"My mother? What about my mother?" I quizzed. I wanted to know exactly how much he knew.

"You said she was killed."

"Nigga, I never told you anything about my mother. What you mean she was killed?" I was playing stupid with him. He didn't know what I knew.

"Somebody shot her. That's what you told me." he continued to talk. All he was doing was digging himself deeper and deeper in a hole.

"You got two seconds to tell me what the fuck you know, or we are going to have an even bigger problem," I muttered.

By then, I'd pulled my gun out of my waist and had it pointed under his chin. He was on some fuck shit. Kosine knew how I was. I'm sure this was not something he was expecting from me. It had to be done. If I kept allowing him to slide with things, he'd never understand where his place was. Underneath me. That was not meant literally either.

"You gonna shoot me? We supposed to be like brothers." Kosine became emotional. I'd never seen that from him. He had to be high. That wasn't a way for this to go down. With him being high, he was an easy target. If anything, I wanted him to be on high alert for what I would've done to him. "I'm sorry, bro. I don't know what I did to you. I'm sorry," he kept apologizing. I removed the gun from under his chin and placed it back in its original home.

"What the fuck is wrong with you? What did you do?" It was as if he were confessing to something without directly coming out and saying what it was. Glancing up at him, I realized his shirt was soaking wet. He was staggering and everything coming out of his mouth was unclear. Tears were running from the corner of his eyes and if I didn't know any better, his ass was slobbering.

"I'm sorry, bro," he said again. This time, he ran a finger down my lips. I pushed his hand out of my face.

"Chill out with that shit. A man doesn't ever need to be touching another man's lips. Especially, not mine," I asserted.

"I'm trying to tell you I'm sorry. I fucked up, bro. You don't know all the shit I've done. I had to do what I did to keep us together. I had your mother killed," he admitted. My mouth dropped. Why was he admitting to the shit? What more did he have to tell me?

"What?" I jumped back, pushing him off me. "You did what?"

"I'm the one that had your mother handled. She hurt you. I was doing it for you. Lyn never would've known about Kazya if it wasn't for her."

"Ko, you better be playing with me nigga."

"She didn't mean shit to you. Why are you acting like you care? You ain't even fuck with her in real life."

"She was my mother. I don't care if I hadn't spoken with her in ten years. She gave me life. She did the best she could to raise me."

"She raised you until you were nine and she didn't do a good job at that. That's why it was easy for the streets to claim you. She didn't love you. Lyn doesn't love you. I'm your brother. I'm the only one that has been in your corner from the jump," he ranted. He held his arms out and came toward me. This fool was trying to give me a damn hug. Yeah, whatever he took had him delusional. Who the hell admits to having your mother murdered and think you're supposed to hug all on them like everything was okay? "Can't you see the reason I did it? Then I have proof that she was feeding information to the police. She was going to have you arrested. You know they been watching your ass. She was more worried about money to supply her drug habit than she was worried about her own son."

"Proof? You always say you have proof for shit but never have anything to show for it. You said the same thing about Day-Day and Yo-Yo. You claim you knew they were the ones coming after me. Yet, I have not seen a single receipt. If you have so much fuckin' proof, produce the shit," I aggressively spoke.

"Fine. I'll get the proof to you. I'll bring the person front and center to you." That sounded like a lie.

"I don't need you bringing anybody to me. I don't trust you at this point. I'm getting the feeling that you're the threat to me."

"Why would I be a threat to you? You're my brother. I love you."

"I'll do you this solid. I'll give you a week to come forward with whatever proof you have that my mother was against me and that Day-Day and Yo-Yo were indeed the people who tried to kill me. If you can't produce these receipts, I'm going to take it as you being the person that's really been after me and I'm going to handle you accordingly," I sternly commented.

Leaving him standing there looking stupid, I hopped in my whip and sped away. Kosine had finally done it. He'd given me all the ammunition I needed to end his ass. It was one thing for him to betray me by sleeping with Lyn. It was something else for him to have my mother killed. Even if she was feeding the police information about me, he should've come to me with what he knew and let me decide how I wanted to handle things. He never gave me that option. He took away the only family I had other than him and Lyn. That's what made me realize that it was his time to go. For his sake, he'd better be able to produce receipts or he wasn't going to have to worry about the crack taking his ass out. I was going to be the one to do it.

## 15

## CORDE' (DAY-DAY)

*ONE WEEK LATER*

Contacting Lyn's family, I knew that I had to get them out of New Orleans. She was going crazy being away from them and they seemed worried out of their mind about her. The way her father used to be in the streets, I had a feeling that Logic wasn't crazy enough to go after him. If he was, he would've done it by now. That would've been his way of being able to get Lyn to come to him. Either that or he was too stupid to think that would work. That was the type of shit that had me wondering why he would be in charge. He made stupid moves for no reason.

"Day-Dayyyyyy?!?" Yo-Yo called out to me. We were standing in the hotel parking lot getting ready to load up and head back to New Orleans. It had been well over a week which I felt was more than enough time for us to get a plan together on how to get rid of Logic and Kosine. We'd actually had eyes on them and were waiting to make our move. Lyn was the only reason I hadn't yet. Something in the back of my mind told me she would hate me if I killed Logic even though she said that it wouldn't bother her.

"You don't hear me calling you?" Yo-Yo said when she was closer to me.

"Yeah, sorry. I was thinking," I admitted to her.

"You don't want to kill him, do you?" she questioned me.

"Kill who?" I replied, acting as if I didn't know what she was talking about.

"You know who I'm talking about. You're worried it's going to mess things up between you and her, aren't you?" Turning my head, I couldn't dare glance into her eyes. I didn't want her reading me and I didn't want her to think I was weak. Yo-Yo placed her hand on the side of my face and turned my head to where I was back facing her.

"It's okay, I understand," she stated.

"No, you don't. For the first time, I've found peace with a woman. That was something I never thought I'd ever find."

"Well damn, what the hell was I?" She giggled.

"You know that's different. You're my sister. You have to love me no matter what happens in our life. It's not like that with her. She has a choice to be with me or not and she's choosing me."

"Day-Day, there are a million and one women on this earth who would choose to be with you. Hell, you've had a ton of them fighting over you," she reminded me. I smiled thinking about the one time I was messing with these two chicks.

I started messing with this eighteen-year-old, Brenda, when I was sixteen and then I ran into this older woman when I was out with her one time. The older woman turned out to be her stepmother, Lacretia. From the beginning, I didn't know that they were related. Brenda asked me to come to her house for dinner one day and that's when I ended up locking eyes with Lacretia. I played it cool the entire time. Lacretia was the one whose face gave it away. She couldn't keep her hands off me. Brenda flew across the table like superman and started beating the brakes off Lacretia. I sat there trying to finish my macaroni and fried chicken while Brenda's father attempted to break the fight up. I probably should've helped him, but I didn't. It wasn't my fight.

They really didn't have a reason to be fighting considering I wasn't in a relationship with either of them. I was their nigga. The nigga they called when they needed a fix. That cuddling and kissing shit was out of the question when it came to me. So, I wasn't even sure what it was that had them hooked, other than me giving them the same big dick energy that I be giving Lyn. The only difference was that the energy I gave Lyn was far more than the energy I'd ever given any other woman in my life. From what I heard, Lacretia and her husband ended up splitting. Brenda was put out of the house for putting her hands on her stepmother. That was all I knew. Following up with them was not something I was interested in doing. It wasn't because I was an asshole. It was simply due to me setting expectations from the jump. If they tried to do anything other than what was discussed that was on them and not my responsibility or fault.

"Bro, get out of your head. Lyn really likes you. I find it hard to believe that she would tell you that she was okay with you handling Logic if she really wasn't. She's not going to leave you. She wants to be with you. I can tell. You need to man the fuck up and let her know what you're feeling so that you can move past this. You know I told you that when you got into this line of work, you can't let anything come in and fuck with your mental. You're doing that right now and that's not going to work with me. If your head is not in the game, it can get us all killed," Yo-Yo practically fussed at me.

"You're right. I'm sorry. I'll talk to her about it before we pull out. Is that all you wanted to talk to me about?" There was no need for me to tell her Lyn and I already had that conversation. She said she was okay with me handling my business. Yet, I still wondered how much it would affect her in the back of my mind.

"No. I needed to let you in on some shit. We gotta make a quick run before we head out," she informed me.

"Quick run? Where? What's going on?" I asked. We had put our plans together on how we were going to get back to New Orleans and get Lyn's parents out of dodge so we could handle business with Kosine and Logic. We were the type of people that once we had our plans together, we stuck to them. The fact that she wanted to deviate from them had me wondering what the hell was going on.

"I got a call from a nigga named Chico. He said he wanted to put us up on game about some shit. I think it's in our best interest to meet up with him," she explained.

"Where do you know him from? Have you met him before?"

"No. I don't know shit about this man. I'm not even sure how he found me."

"That's strange as hell. You didn't have your old phone on you so how the hell he get in touch with you?" She was saying shit that made sense to her but wasn't adding up to me. I needed to know what the hell was going on and as quickly as possible.

"While we were out getting clothes the other day, I stopped inside of Verizon and got another phone. Different phone, same number. I changed all of my passwords and shit so I couldn't be tracked."

"That's cool and shit, but how the hell the nigga get your number. Anybody who's ever had to get in touch with us had a process."

"Damn, you nosey. I thought you would've trusted my judgement and shit by now." She stopped speaking and stepped in closer to me. "He didn't exactly call my phone. He went through the same process anyone else would when they wanted us to take care of somebody. This time when he placed the call for us to handle business, he wanted us to take care of a mutual friend," she explained.

"Who?"

"Kosine."

"What? Somebody is actually paying us to take that nigga out?"

"Yes. I think we should check into it," she advised me. If Yo-Yo felt good about it, I had no reason to doubt her. That meant she'd already ran a check to make sure the nigga was legit before she even came to me about it.

"Aight. What are we going to tell them?" I asked, pointing toward the hotel. It was only a matter of time before Mercury and Lyn would come galloping out of the hotel, ready to go. I'd promised Lyn today would be the day. I'd hate to have to go back on my word to her.

"You ain't got to tell them shit. Tell them that we have to make a pitstop and let that be it."

"You know like I know that Lyn is going to start questioning me. I can't lie to her. If I tell one lie, she's going to hold that shit over my head forever."

"Boy, you are pussy whipped like a mufucka. I've never known you to act like this over a bitch. You need to get it together. She knows the type of work you're in. She's going to have to suck the shit up and take whatever the fuck you tell her," Yo-Yo fussed.

"Who has to take whatever you tell them?" I heard Lyn's voice. Yo-Yo and I were so deep in conversation, that neither of us saw them coming toward us.

"It's work shit," Yo-Yo told her and walked around to the other side of the car.

"What is she talking about?" Lyn questioned me. For some reason, she was not buying the shit that Yo-Yo had said.

"Someone reached out that may know something about Kosine. Yo-Yo wants to meet with him," I blurted out. There was no reason for me to lie to her.

"Fine. Let's go," Lyn emphasized.

"Excuse me?" I asked, wanting to be sure I heard her correctly.

"You heard me. This has got to end. Getting rid of Kosine means you'll be closer to getting rid of Logic. I'm ready for my life to go back to as normal as I can possibly get it," she quipped.

"Chill out, Killa. You're not about to take yourself out here and end up getting hurt. Yo-Yo and I got this."

"No, the fuck you don't. I've sat by for far too long allowing other people to be in control of what's going on with and around me. I'm tired of it. If he knows something, I want to know what he knows."

"Do you hear this shit, Yo-Yo?" I said over my shoulder.

"She's right. Besides, if she is going to be with you, she needs to have a backbone. There's no better time than the present for her to grow one," Yo-Yo agreed with her. All I could do was sigh. It seemed that they were teamed up with each other. There was nothing more I could say. Lyn had made her mind up. That was clear when she moved around me and hopped inside the car as if I weren't trying to convince her to change her mind.

"What about your parents?" I asked Lyn. Saying that was my hope that she would think about them and change her mind about what she wanted to do.

"What about them? They are grown. My father has been in the streets and I'm sure he is very capable of taking care of himself and my mother. They can wait. Let's go handle this shit," she instructed before slamming her door. Running my hand down my face, I jogged over to the driver's side and got in the car.

"Where are we headed?" I asked Yo-Yo who was sitting in the front seat grinning like the shit was funny.

"The address is already entered," she replied. She placed her airpods in her ears and leaned her seat back.

Checking my rearview mirror, I noticed both Mercury and Lyn sitting in the backseat with a worried expression on their face. Mercury, I could care less about. For some reason, I felt as though I was taking Lyn inside of a lion's den. If something were to happen to her, I was kicking Yo-Yo's ass. Sister or not.

## 16

# CHICO

Kosine fucked up when he put his hands on me. After everything I'd done to help him, that was the way he chose to repay me. It was wrong. He had no business going near my family. The best way for me to handle the situation was for me to get rid of his ass. He had to feel my wrath. Let me explain why I'm even in this situation.

Kosine and I did a bid together when we were younger. I'd gotten arrested for breaking and entering. I was scared as hell when I got to juvie. All the other boys saw that shit and tried to come at me. Kosine didn't. He said it was because he saw potential in me. He basically took me under his wing and trained me to be what he wanted me to be. We were young but nobody fucked with me because they were scared of Kosine. He didn't rape me but there were times when he'd have me sucking his dick. He said it wasn't gay if we didn't penetrate each other. Nobody ever knew what happened between us. We were supposed to take it to the grave, but that shit changed.

We were separated when we reached eighteen. He was sent to an adult jail and I was released. I think it was because his charge was more severe than mine. He was in trouble for attempted murder or something along those lines. I'm sure that played a major factor in the reason the other boys in juvie were afraid of him. At the time we were there, nobody had a charge as severe as his. In the midst of us being separated, Kosine told me that I owed him for always having his back. I believed him.

A few months ago, he hit me up and was telling me that he was having problems out of Logic. I hated to hear it considering the talk on the street was about how close they were. He convinced me that the talk was all fake and that Logic was not who he said he was. Kosine agreed to pay me enough money to get my family out of the projects if I would help him take Logic out. Not working and having additional mouths to feed meant that I had to do any and everything I could to provide for my family. Naturally, I took the offer. That was the worse decision I'd ever made in my life. Kosine got to a point of thinking he controlled me. Every move I made; he had a problem with it. He constantly made threats to harm me or my family when he didn't get the response or reaction he wanted out of me. It was crazy. I made up in my mind that I needed to take Logic out, get my money, and get the hell out of dodge.

The first attempt to take Logic out was when he was leaving the strip club one night. While they were inside, I got close enough to their car to loosen all the lug nuts and cut the damn break lines. Leave it to Logic to want to leave with Kazya's ass. He had someone from his crew drive his car home. They ended up meeting the fate that was meant for Logic. Since that didn't go as planned, Kosine came up with the idea to tell Logic that it was Day-Day and Yo-Yo that were trying to take him out. That was when they came up with the plan to fake his death. The only option I had was to help him make the shit seem real. That kept both Kosine and I free of Logic's wrath if he were to learn that we were really the ones behind trying to kill him.

***Ring... Ring... Ring...***

The ringing of my phone removed me from my thoughts. When I glanced down and saw that it was coming from an unknown number, I answered. I knew exactly who it had to be. I couldn't wait to tell them everything that had transpired so that Kosine would have to pay for all the shit he put me through.

"Hello," I cheerfully answered

"Fuck you so happy about?" Yo-Yo asked through the phone. That made me change my voice up to not seem so happy.

"My bad... Are you close by?"

"We're out here. Where are you?"

"I'm on the beach standing by the Phoenix West Condos," I advised her.

"Pull your hands out of your pocket and pull your pockets out," she directed me. Slowly, I moved and did everything that she asked.

"Put your hands in the air and don't make any sudden movements," she continued.

Raising my arms above my head, I felt someone come up from behind me and begin to pat me down. They moved from my neck all the way down to my shoes. I was pissed when they found the mini pistol I kept in my damn sock.

"Smart ass," a male's voice stated.

"Hey Day-Day," I greeted him.

"Don't say my mufuckin' name," he grunted and pushed me out toward the beach.

"Don't kill me," I begged even though I didn't know if that was his intention or not.

"Ain't nobody about to kill your dumb ass unless you on some bullshit. That's not what you're on, are you?" Day-Day asked me.

"No. Absolutely not. I'm trying to help ya'll so you can help me," I asserted. That was the honest to God truth.

Day-Day had something poking at my back as we continued to walk. We walked until we came up on two women. I'd seen both of the women before. One was Yo-Yo for sure. The other was the woman that I always saw with Logic.

"Hey Yo-Yo. You must be Logic's wife," I greeted them both.

"Don't call me that," Logic's wife muttered, dropping her head.

"This not about her. Tell me what the fuck you wanted to meet about, nigga," Day-Day angrily spat.

"This is about her. All of this is about her. Don't you get it?" I emphasized to him. I didn't understand why it was so hard for them to see that Lyn was the piece of the puzzle that was controlling the chain of events happening in their lives.

"How? How is this all about me?" Lyn asked.

"Kosine wants you. The fact that he hasn't been able to get you is what's sparked all of this shit," I called myself explaining.

"Keep going. Tell us everything and don't leave shit out," Yo-Yo ordered.

Once she opened the door for me to tell her everything, that's exactly what I did. From telling her how I met him to telling her about the latest attempt on Logic's life. I told her about Kosine having Logic's mother killed because she knew too much about what Kosine had been doing. I was the one that had been supplying her with the drugs. When Logic became curious and started digging deeper into things, Kosine stated she had to go. That was why he ended her life the way that he did. He got someone to kill her. The initial plan was to allow her to overdose on some bad drugs. Logic had gotten too close so he couldn't risk her not dying when he needed her to. The two shots, one to the head and one to the chest, was all it took to shut her up for good.

"Where's his wife and kids?" Lyn asked. That caught me off guard. Why would she wonder about them when she clearly didn't give a fuck about his kids?

"Why you asking about them?" I curiously asked her.

"I have a damn heart. I'd never want anything to happen to the kids even though I didn't fuck with their mother. They didn't ask to be here nor is it their fault that they were brought into this crazy situation. Are they okay?"

"They are fine. Kazya might not be so lucky when it's all said and done. Like I said, Kosine is making it a point to leave no stones unturned. If there is anyone out there that can tell Logic what's really going on, Kosine is trying to take them out one by one."

"So where is she?" Lyn asked again.

"Kosine told me to kill her. I couldn't. I grew up without a mother and didn't want that for the kids. When we had her take the kids to his mother's house, I told him that I killed her. I really have her hiding out somewhere in Florida."

"The kids?"

"The kids are with the social workers. When his mother was killed, there was no one there to get the kids. Kazya couldn't come out of hiding or she was as good as dead."

"You mean to tell me that Logic's dumb ass didn't care enough to come out to get his own kids? What kind of shit is that?"

"He's a selfish man. If it doesn't involve him, his money, or you, he ain't fuckin' with it. Why you think he did Kazya the way that he did? She's not you," I expressed.

"Damn... You must be sprinkling fairy dust on these niggas through your pussy to have them going crazy like that," Yo-Yo joked to Lyn. She was the only one who found it funny.

"Really Yo-Yo?" Day-Day chided.

"My bad, bro. I'm trying to make light of the situation. This is crazy. We've never had to deal with anything this fucked up," she stated.

"Neither have I," I told them.

"Why are you telling us all of this?" Lyn questioned me.

"Do you see what this nigga did to me? I told him that after we failed several times at getting rid of Logic that I didn't want any parts of it. All I wanted him to do was give me some of the money he owed me and allow me to get the hell out of dodge with my family. That wasn't good enough for him. He beat my ass and did something to my baby's mother and daughter. I can't stand for that. I need him gone so that I can get my family back," I admitted to them.

"Wow. If it weren't for that, you wouldn't have told us

anything, huh?" Lyn acknowledged. All I could do was drop my head. She was right. If things would've gone the way I wanted them to go then I would've been out of dodge and my mouth would've remained shut.

"Call him," Day-Day stated.

"Call who?" I quizzed.

"Call Kosine, nigga," he demanded.

"For what? I don't need him to know that I told y'all anything. He has my family. He'll kill them," I expressed.

"Not once did I tell you to call and tell him you were with us. Call him out of concern for your family. See if you can meet up with him. You better make the shit sound believable or he's going to be gunning for your head," Day-Day emphasized. He was right. If I called and acted like I was worried about my family, which I was, Kosine would believe it. He would talk to me and I'd probably be able to get him to meet up with me. I wished there was a way I could have Logic there during the meet up so he'd be able to see who was really behind trying to kill him. That was a risk I couldn't take. The minute Kosine spotted Logic, he was going to put things together and my family would be as good as dead. I couldn't afford for that to happen. Not because of me. I'd never be able to live with myself with their blood on my hands.

"Fine," I agreed, quickly dialing Kosine's number.

"Fuck you want?" Kosine bellowed into the phone once I dialed his number.

"I want to meet up with you," I told him.

"Meet up with me for what?"

"We need to talk about my family. I've done everything you asked me to do. There was no need for you to go after them the way that you did." My anger began to intensify. Thoughts of seeing Kosine take his last breath was the only thing running through my mind at that time.

"Nigga, fuck you!" Kosine stated and began chuckling.

"This shit's not funny. Meet me or I'm going to tell Logic

everything," I found the courage to say. I was nervous as hell. Being in the streets was not new to me. This killing shit was. That's why I failed miserably at it. I wasn't even sure why Kosine thought I'd be able to do the shit in the first place. He needed a crash dummy and I fed right into the bullshit.

"Aight. That's fine. Where are you?"

"Naw. I'm going to text you when and where. The ball is in my court right now."

"You know that I have your two bitches, right? I wouldn't keep playing with me if I were you. You poppin' big shit and making threats but all you're doing is digging a bigger hole for your family and an even bigger one for yourself. Play with me if you mufuckin' want to and see won't you find bits and pieces of their bodies leading to decapitated heads," he roared. My mouth snapped shut. He was not playing. My eyes darted over to Day-Day and Yo-Yo who shrugged their shoulders. They were the ones who wanted me to call and now they didn't have shit to say. That was fucked up.

"What do you want from me, Ko?"

"I want that nigga Logic dead and I want him dead tonight."

"I can't do it tonight."

"You'd better mufuckin' do it or you will never see your family again."

"Where will he be? How will I get to him?"

"I'll take him back to the house in Atlanta. We'll be there by seven tonight. Have your ass there and be ready to handle his ass. I want this to end tonight," he chided and ended the call. From the way he was talking, I knew his teeth were clenched together. It was sad how much anger and rage he had when it came down to Logic and they were supposed to be family. The jealousy and greed were too much.

"What now?" I asked Day-Day.

"You're going to that house."

"Are you crazy? I can't kill Logic?"

"We don't want you to. We want you to confront Kosine in

front of him. All of this shit needs to come to the light. Once you speak your peace, we'll handle the rest," Yo-Yo chimed in.

For a brief moment, I felt things might be alright. With Yo-Yo and Day-Day both there to have my back, what could go wrong?

## 17

## EVELYN (LYN)

Standing there, I took in everything Chico said to Kosine on the phone. He was putting more trust into Kosine than he needed to. Something told me in my gut that Kosine was not about to have Logic available when Chico showed up so Chico could take him out. He was setting Chico up to kill him because he'd become a threat to him.

"Lyn?" Corde' said my name, causing me to snap out of the trance I was in.

"I'd hate to get you involved in this, but I need you," he said.

"You're not getting me involved in anything that Logic and Kosine didn't already have me involved in. Whatever you need me to do, I'll do it. Just tell me what it is," I told him, meaning every word.

"What is she going to do? She's not a match against them," Chico chimed in.

"I don't have to be a match for them. One thing you fail to realize is that if I told Logic that I wanted to be with him, he is going to believe it. He'd kill you before he kills me. I have a better chance of bringing him out of hiding than you do," I honestly spoke.

"Yeah. Whatever."

"Don't get a funky attitude with me because you scared. How you a grown ass man but you are letting another man punk you? Both of y'all walking around here with a bat and two balls and you're still scared of him."

"I'm not scared of no damn body. I'm worried about my family." He appeared hostile.

"Then you need to take all that hostility and anger that you have against him and use that shit to your advantage," I advised him. "Let's go," I told Corde'.

"Hold up, baby. We are all going together," Corde' advised me.

"I'm not getting into a car with him. For all we know, Kosine been watching his ass this entire time. He can get killed on his own time. He knows where we are supposed to be meeting up later tonight. All that riding together shit is unnecessary." I sounded like a bitch but that was not my intention. I had to do what was best for me at some point. This was the perfect time for me to start.

"You letting her tell you what to do like that? Damn. You just as weak as Logic is," Chico commented. I opened my mouth to address him, but Corde' threw his hand up to stop me.

"It's not about being weak. She's my woman. She's like a rare jewel and I've noticed that about her. She's not going to lead me astray. She has my back like I have hers. She's right about your toxic ass. You bad luck nigga. We not 'bout to risk our lives to help some pussy ass nigga that has us in this damn situation because he couldn't stand up to Kosine. Now, the next time you decide to bad mouth a bitch, you need to make sure it's not mine or you won't have to worry about Kosine killing you. I will," Corde' spat.

"That's right, bitch!" I sassed. I rolled my eyes and turned my head close enough to him that my hair slapped him in the face. Grabbing Corde's hand, we headed back to the car. From my peripheral, I could see Mercury, Yo-Yo, and Chico following close behind. When we got near the car, I noticed Corde' starting to slow down.

"What's wrong?" I asked. My nerves got the best of me. I began to survey our surroundings to see if there was anything off.

"We need to go ahead and call Logic. I need to make sure he's going to be at the spot tonight."

"You're going to kill him tonight?" I inquired.

"We might not have to kill him. With any luck, him and Kosine will kill each other when he finds out what's really going on," Corde' announced.

"So, what do you need me to do?"

"He needs your smart ass to call Logic and make sure he's there. What part of that don't you get?" Mercury snapped.

"Bitch, I know the fuck you lyin'," Yo-Yo stepped in and stated. "Don't get fucked up talking to my sister like that. We told you we'd do what we could to help you find your daughter which is the only reason we're letting your hating ass roll with us. If you come at her or any of us sideways again, I'm going to personally slit your throat and dump your body in a landfill like the trash that you are," Yo-Yo added.

"Sister? You don't even know her a-"

***Bow...***

Mercury never got the chance to get out whatever she was trying to say. Yo-Yo punched her dead in the mouth. Mercury's hand swiftly flew to her mouth.

"You bitch," she said after a while. Mercury charged at Yo-Yo. She was wildly swinging her hands. Yo-Yo stuck her hand out and placed it on Mercury's forehead. Since Yo-Yo was bigger and stronger, Mercury never got a chance to connect with her. She was standing there swinging her arms like a mad woman. She started to tire out and Yo-Yo noticed it. Yo-Yo stood there giggling the entire time before she finally decided to let Mercury go. Mercury fell forward and landed in the sand. She laid there for a while before she stood up, spat out the sand that had gotten in her mouth and dusted herself off.

"You want to fight me?" Yo-Yo asked her. "I promise you that I can give you an ass whooping worse than that shit Kosine used to do to your ass," Yo-Yo warned her.

"Mercury, please let it go. We are trying to get out of this mess so we can all go our separate ways. You need us to help you find Jovi. Don't piss them off and they refuse to help you. You'll be screwed," I reminded her.

"Fine. I'm beating her ass later," Mercury grunted and stomped toward the car.

Corde' just had to be petty. He unlocked his side of the door and got inside the car. He leaned over and unlocked the door for Yo-Yo to get in and she leaned back and opened the door for me. Corde' crank the car and was about to drive off. Mercury stood outside the car beating on the window.

"She can ride with Chico," Yo-Yo seethed.

"What? She could get killed." I practically pleaded with them to let her in the car with us.

"So? She needs to learn who to and who not to cross. I'm that bitch, but I'm NOT THAT BITCH!" Yo-Yo stated.

"Huh? What does that even mean?"

"It means I'm the bitch in these streets but I'm also not the bitch you want to cross. She has come at all of us wrong one too many times. She needs to learn the power of respect." Yo-Yo rolled her window down and instructed Mercury to get in the car with Chico. Mercury knew that could've sealed her destiny. She stood outside the car we were in crying and begging them to let her inside.

"Baby, please let her in. She has a child," I said to Corde'.

"She needs to learn her lesson, Lyn. I'm sorry." He wouldn't budge. There was nothing more I could say or do. I mouthed to Mercury that I was sorry.

"Either get in the car with Chico or stay your dumb ass here," Corde' told her.

It took some time. Mercury finally realized that Corde' and

Yo-Yo weren't going to change their mind. She went ahead and got in the car with Chico.

"I can't believe you did that," I told Corde'.

"Well, believe it. I told you that something is not right with that girl. She's selfish. She came at you and I both wrong. She has to deal with what she did," Yo-Yo snarled.

"Not like this," I said.

"Then how? You suggest we leave her where Kosine could get to her again? She's not dead. She's not going to die. We got this. Let us do what the fuck we do and stop questioning us. Damn!" Yo-Yo chided.

"Chill out, sis. You know you can't talk to her like that," Corde' finally spoke up for me.

"Then you need to handle your bitch."

"No. I'm going to handle your mufuckin' ass if you don't watch your fuckin' mouth. Don't start this shit," he told her.

"Whatever. Drive," she instructed him.

Although hesitant, Corde' put the car in drive and we started heading back toward Georgia. We were riding in silence until Yo-Yo turned around and handed me a phone.

"Make the call," she told me. I knew what she wanted so there was no need for me to act like I didn't. I wanted to get this shit over and done with as quickly as possible.

Dialing his number, I patiently waited for him to answer. When he did, my words seemingly were caught in my throat. I didn't know what to say or do.

"Say something..." Yo-Yo whispered.

"Lo-Lo-Logic?" I softly spoke into the phone.

"Lyn?" he called out my name.

"Hey! It's me," I told him.

"Baby girl, where are you? I'm sorry for putting my hands on you. We can work it out," he pleaded with me. It sounded sincere and convincing, but I knew him. He was trying to rope me in more than I was trying to rope him in.

"Can we meet and talk?" I asked.

"Meet me at the house," he stated.

"The house? The one you were holding me at?"

"No. Our house. The house that belongs to us. The one we vowed to spend the rest of our lives in," he informed me and hung the phone up.

"What the fuck!" I bellowed. "Why does he want me to go there? What about Chico and setting up Kosine? What are we supposed to do now?" I asked a thousand questions hoping and praying that Corde' or Yo-Yo could give me answers.

"He knows what he's doing. We'll have to get Chico to reroute Kosine to that same house," Yo-Yo advised us.

"Why? Why there?" I asked again.

"He wants to go back to where it all started. Put your seat belt on. We are going to end this shit where it never should've begun," Corde' announced.

Sitting back, my nerves quickly shot to ten. I didn't know what was going to happen. Whatever it was, was not going to be good. Silently, I prayed that I'd make it out alive.

# 18

## KOSINE

***Ring... Ring... Ring...***

"Who dis?" I answered my phone for what seemed like the umpteenth time. It was ringing off the hook with people calling and asking to take me on dates, moaning through the phone, or holding the bitch and breathing into it.

"Is this Kosine?" a husky, yet raspy voice said on the other line.

"Who dis?" I asked again.

"This is Kentrell."

"Kentrell who?"

"Why so many questions?"

"Nigga, don't be calling my phone and not properly announcing yourself," I grunted. I didn't want nobody playing on my damn phone and wasting my unlimited minutes. The fuck was that nigga on?

"Calm down. I got a question for you since you want to do so much talking," the nigga stated without answering my question.

"Nigga, what the fuck you want?"

"You ever been to the chocolate factory?" he asked out of nowhere. It threw me off. What the hell kind of question was that?

"What damn chocolate factory? I ain't never even heard of no shit like that," I seethed.

"Well, you can forget my name is Kentrell and call me Willy Wonka. I'm trying to take you to the chocolate factory and fill you with all the chocolate your heart desires," he cooed. I could tell he was happy to say that to me by the high pitch in his tone. He had to have practiced that shit. It was too stupid to be something he'd just made up.

"What nigga? Are you fuckin' coming on to me?" I was in utter disbelief. He had to be out of his fuckin' mind.

"I'm trying to give you what you wanted. I have a few friends I can bring along. With the five of us, we'll have no problems taking you down," he blurted out.

"You trying to die, I see."

"Die? For trying to please you?" He made his last statement before getting quiet. "Oh, you meant you trying to kill me with that D, huh? I don't see how. You are a little small down there, but I can work with it," the nigga had the nerve to say.

"Fuck you ole bitch ass nigga. Call my phone again and I'm scattering your brains out in front of your mufuckin' mammy," I threatened before ending the call.

Sitting in my car, my mind was racing. With all of the strange calls I'd been getting, it had me wondering if they were all linked to that Facebook account. It was nobody but Mercury behind the shit.

***Ring... Ring... Ring...***

"Who dis" I answered again.

"You lookin' for a good time, baby?" *Is this nigga trying to hit on me too*, I thought. The shit was sickening. If that was how they picked women up, they needed better pick-up lines because the shit was sad. After a few more calls, I went to my settings and changed it to where any number that was not stored in my phone was sent to voicemail. It was either that or change my number. Changing my number was not an option.

There I sat in my car, contemplating over what my next

move needed to be. I glanced down and noticed the time on my phone. It reminded me that I was supposed to link up with Chico. Yet, I needed to make sure Logic was nowhere to be found when I did. I picked up my phone and was getting ready to call Logic, but the phone started ringing as soon as I did.

"Yo?" I stated to Chico once I'd answered.

"Change of plans," Chico said.

"What? You not running this show, I am. What the hell you mean by a change of plans?"

"Word on the street is that Logic is headed back to New Orleans. That's where I'm headed."

"What the hell you mean by word on the street? Logic don't tell people his moves unless he telling me. What makes you think you can get on the phone and tell me what the hell to do?" I roared. I felt myself becoming angrier and angrier at the way he'd attempted to handle me.

"Let me show you something," Chico stated and got quiet. My phone alerted me of a text, so I removed it from my ear to check it. It was a text from Chico.

"Why are you texting me when we are on the phone? You can tell me whatever the hell it is you need to say," I informed him.

"Shut up and check the message," he told me.

Hesitantly, I opened the message. All I saw was red. I did a double take to make sure my eyes weren't deceiving me. They weren't. Sitting straight up and proud in his front seat was Mercury.

"Nigga, what the fuck you doing with my bitch?" I grunted through the phone.

"You got mine, so I got yours," he quipped.

"That shit don't move me. Your bitch means more to you than that bitch means to me. You can keep her ass," I retorted.

"You sure about that? She knows your every move. She knows about your business. She's more of a liability than anything for you, I have no problem keeping her. I'm warning you that if I do, I'm going straight to the police station with her, my nigga. You think you're laughing now. I can assure you that I'll get the last laugh," he concluded.

Chico was right. I'd gotten comfortable around Mercury. I figured she'd always be there. There was no reason for me to hide anything from her. Had I known there was a chance that we'd be in the position we were in today, then I wouldn't have allowed her to know so much about my operation. She knew too much. She was definitely a liability and had to be dealt with. I wanted to be the one to do it.

"Fine. When and where?"

"We're headed back to New Orleans."

"For what? I'm not nowhere near there."

"I suggest you head back that way. I want you to go back to the same place you went to when you killed my brother," Chico mumbled.

"Brother? Who the fuck is your brother?" I questioned confused as to what he was talking about.

"Rae, mufucka. That was my brother. I've been waiting for this day for a long time. You think us linking up again was a coincidence? It was only a matter of time before your greed got the best of you and you were going to need someone outside of your circle to help you complete your deed of taking over. I waited in limbo for you to start asking around. That was the perfect chance for me to get someone to remind you of our bid in juvie together. You came to me because you thought I owed you for protecting me when we were younger. It's funny how small the world is. I'm not as weak as you think I am. I was playing a part. Now, it's your time to pay the piper. You and this bitch. My brother's blood is on your hands. You drained him of his blood and now I'm about to drain you of yours. Meet me at the same place you killed him at," he demanded and ended the call. That caused me to chuckle. Chico decided to grow some damn balls. That was quite flattering. Too bad it was a little too late and it was going to cause him his life in the end.

The need for backup was real. Therefore, I had no choice

but to make the dreaded call. As the phone rang, I ran many statements through my mind that I could tell him to get the help I was going to need. The most logical thing to say was the thing I hated to say the most. Yet, with it halfway being the truth, it may help to get the situation to work out in my favor.

"Yeah?" Logic answered the phone giving me a lot of attitude.

"Take that bass out of your voice when you talking to me," I fussed.

"I don't have time for your shit. If you not about to give me the information I asked for, we don't have shit to discuss."

"That's what I'm calling you for. I found out the person really responsible for the shooting. He told me that he was coming for all of us."

"Who?"

"I don't think you know him. That nigga crazy though. We got to handle this situation ASAP," I emphasized.

"Who?" he asked again.

"I told you I don't think you know him. Some street nigga that they said going after everybody territory," I lied.

"Nigga, say who the fuck it is or get the fuck off my line. I don't have time for you to be dancing around the subject. I need to end this shit now!" he roared.

"Aight. Damn! The nigga's name is Chico. He from Florida or some shit. He headed to our neck of the woods trying to take over the streets. He's managed to take over from everybody but us. So, he's been doing his best to take us down. They are starting with you and plan to work their way down through the whole crew."

***Bam...***

Logic slammed his hand down on something. I heard it through the phone. It almost caused me to jump. However, I expected the anger and rage for him. I would've been the same way.

"I need eyes and ears on him now. I got to find out where he is so I can end this shit tonight," he advised me.

"I know where he is. He called and made a threat to me a few seconds ago."

"Spit it out. Where is he?"

"He wants me to meet him in New Orleans at the house Mercury's mother used to live in," I explained.

"Why there?" he queried.

"I don't know. I'm 'bout to pull out now and head that way. This must be his attempt to get rid of me since he has failed at every attempt to get rid of you," I stated.

"That don't sound right. I ain't never even heard of that nigga. He ain't got no reason to come for me," he seethed.

"You're the man in these streets. Everybody got a reason to come for you."

"Even you?" he snidely replied.

"This ain't the time for you to start throwing your balls around. You've told me who was in charge and I get it," I lied. I couldn't argue with him because he'd start to question me more and I didn't need that, not right now. I wanted to get him to the spot to take Chico out and finally go ahead and get rid of his ass. With any luck, they'd engage in a shootout and kill each other.

"Where this nigga meeting you at?" he asked again.

"At Mercury's mother's house," I repeated.

"What? Why there?" he queried once more.

"That's where I killed that nigga, Rae," I finally admitted.

"Wait... You told me that Rae was killed by Day-Day. What the fuck is going on?"

When those words left his mouth, I clammed up. I'd forgotten that I told him that. Damn. I needed to stop lying. I learned a long time ago that when you tell one lie, you have to tell another lie to cover that one up. I was fuckin' myself up big time.

"It's a long story. That's neither here nor there. He was fuckin' my bitch and I had to end his ass. All I need is for you to have my back. I don't care when you've been wrong, I was there for you. Do the same for me." The line was quiet. He was more than likely thinking of another question to ask me or some way to belittle me and try to make me feel like shit. It was bad enough that he didn't realize by now that the only people I cared about was Lyn and my damn self. The rest of these people could go to hell.

"Aight. I was headed there anyway. Send me the address and I'll hit you up as soon as I touch down." He said what he said and hung up without giving me the chance to ask any questions. I wanted to know why he said he was headed to New Orleans. He had no reason to be going there unless he was up to something. I was determined to find out what it was.

With my mind on Lyn and us getting the chance to finally be together, I rushed to get on the road. I hit up some of the homies I knew rocked with me to tell them what was up and have them meet me at the spot as well. I didn't know what Chico was up to. Whatever it was, I wasn't about to be blindsided.

## 19

## MERCURY

My eyes bucked when I heard Chico mention that Rae was his brother. I never knew Rae even had a brother. That showed how well you can know a person. We'd fucked around for years only for me to see that what I thought was love, had to only be lust for me to never have met his family or know much about his background.

"Why you looking like that?" Chico asked me with an evil grin on his face.

"What are you going to do to me?" I asked, moving uncomfortably in my seat.

"The same thing y'all did to my brother. You think I don't know that you're the reason he's dead?"

"It's not my fault. I wasn't the one who killed him." I tried reasoning with him. The way that he was talking let me know that his mind was made up and he was not trying to hear anything I had to say. I continued to pray that he would hear me out. I needed him too. Why would he want to leave his niece without both of her parents?

"It is your fault. You think Kosine doesn't like to talk when he gets high? That nigga told me everything from how your mother played you and got you to bring your dumb ass back this way to how he killed my brother. If my brother took you away, I know his intentions were pure and he did everything he could to keep you safe. You begged him to take you back home. He did it because he loved you. That love for you left him dead and you're still breathing. You deserve everything Kosine has ever done to your bitch ass," he spat.

Chico continued to ramble on and on about some shit I didn't understand. All I wanted was for his ass to let me go. He played the role of a bitch very well. Who would've thought that he wasn't as scared as he pretended to be?

"That meant you had all of this planned out. You knew that Day-Day and Yo-Yo would jump on board with helping you get rid of Kosine."

"Why wouldn't they? Nobody likes the nigga but your dumb ass. Everyone in the city would be better off with him being dead."

"I loved Rae. I would have never done anything to hurt him," I cried.

"Yet again, you're here and he's not," he snarled.

"What about Jovi?"

"What about her? I know where she is. She'll be well taken care of. You think I would let something happen to my brother's only child? Unlike you, I know how to protect the things and people I love," he told me.

"You can't know how to protect them if you allowed Kosine to come in like a thief in the night and take your baby momma and child," I countered, trying to get under his skin.

"Girl, please. I don't know them damn folks. I paid that bitch to act like we were a fuckin' couple and that was my child. The shit people do for money."

"You'd let an innocent woman and child die over your own selfish motivation?"

"The woman knew what she was getting herself into. I'm not worried about Kosine killing the child. He's not that vicious. Think about it... He learned that Jovi wasn't his. He may have made threats against her life, but he has never hurt her. He is not as cold hearted as you think he is."

"He's not that cold hearted? He beat me every chance that he got. How is that not cold hearted?"

"Do me a favor... Pull that visor down," he instructed me. Moving slowly, I did what he requested. "Now, slide that cover back off the mirror." Again, I did what he said. "Stare in that mirror and tell me who's looking back at you," he commented.

"What do you mean? It's my reflection. I'm looking at me."

"Case proven. You think these folks worried about your ass, Mercury? Why the hell you think they told you to ride with me when they knew I had a target on my back? You can't possibly be as slow as you act," he chided.

"Aagggghhhh..." Rage filled my body; I was so tired of people talking to me crazy. I was tired of being everybody's punching bag. I mustered up as much strength as I could and proceeded to swing on Chico. The car began swerving in and out of lanes. Other cars passing by were blowing their horns at us to let him know that he was going in their lane. We could have had an accident, but I didn't care. That would be my chance to escape.

***Wamp...***

Continuously swinging my arms, I was finally able to connect with Chico's head.

***Thump...***

"Get the fuck off me." Chico slapped me so hard that my head flew back and hit the passengers' side window.

"Muthafu-" I raised my hand and was getting ready to hit him again. My actions were halted.

***Click... Click...***

"Go right ahead. Hit me and risk never seeing Jovi again," he warned me. Pulling over on the side of the road, he turned to face me. Not once did he put the gun down.

"Why are you doing this?"

"Bitch, I ain't done shit to you. I'm taking you back to your man."

"You want to kill me?"

"Did I say I was killing you or was the plan to kill him?" He was right. He never actually said he was going to kill me, but I wasn't a fool. He had to avenge his brother's death. If it weren't for me, Rae would still be amongst the living. That would be his reason for killing me and I couldn't say that I blamed him. Kosine was the one who actually caused him to take his last breath so I could understand the way he felt toward him and his desire for wanting him dead. Everything that I had done was coming back on me.

"I'll do whatever you want. We can be a family together. You, me, and Jovi. We can live out Rae's dreams of her growing up in a two-parent household. All he ever wanted was for Jovi to be loved and treated right. We can give her that." At that point, I was willing to say or do anything that I needed to say in order to make sure I stayed alive.

"Shut up, Mercury. I don't want your ass. You aren't the type of woman that a man makes his wife. Even if you were, I would never be with you."

"Why?"

"You were with my brother. That's nasty as fuck!"

"Whatever. I don't like you anyway."

"Mercury, for your sake and mine, sit the fuck back and shut up. We have a long drive and I promise I don't want to hear your mouth the whole ride," he demanded and pulled back out into traffic.

My nerves were on a thousand as we drove. There was so much I wanted to say. Yet, I didn't speak. Hearing my voice would make him angrier and I couldn't risk it. Not if I wanted a chance to see Jovi again.

"Here, get something to drink," he told me after us driving for a while.

"I'm not thirsty," I stated, turning down his kind gesture.

"Did I ask you if you were thirsty or did I tell you to drink this?" he grunted.

"I'm sorry," I apologized and cowered in the seat like I always did with Kosine. Taking the water bottle from his hand, I opened it up and took a small swig.

"Drink a little more," he demanded and winked at me. I clearly didn't move fast enough for him because he put his hand under the bottle and pushed it up so that the water would go rushing into my mouth. It was flowing in so fast I started choking.

"Don't waste my shit," he fussed. He was raising his voice at me and it was his fault that it was spilling out. Shaking his head, he pulled his hand back. I used that as my chance to put the bottle down.

Using the back of my hand, I wiped my mouth. My shirt was drenched with water. Abruptly, I sat up. My head was spinning, and my heart rate increased. Something was wrong.

"What did you give me?"

"It doesn't matter. Rest easy, Ma." Those were the last words I heard before my breathing slowed. My chest moved up and down at a snail's pace. I clawed at the door handle praying I could get it open and get out of the car. I couldn't.

Nothing that I tried worked. Chico had poisoned me. He said he wanted revenge for his brother's death. He meant that shit. It was sad that I had to be the first one to go.

## 20

## CHICO

What? Before people get into an uproar, they had to understand that I had a role to play. You can't come for my family and think you'd be allowed to get away with it. My brother didn't do anything to anybody. The only fault he had was loving Mercury's bitch ass. I'm sure Kosine was hoping that nobody would tell what he did. However, he had to know that people talked. Hell, nobody talked more than him. He always felt like he had to brag to make himself seem bigger than he was. I knew the truth. I knew he wasn't shit.

Killing Mercury was never in my original plans. However, the more I thought about my brother and replayed in my mind the story Kosine told me about how he killed him, I had no choice but to get rid of her. The whole time she was thinking that Kosine had Jovi, he didn't. Crossing paths with Kosine, I was able to convince him the best way to control Mercury was to take something from her that she loved. As long as Jovi was out of her reach, Mercury would fall in line. There was no denying she loved Jovi and would do whatever she had to do to make sure she was safe. Kosine agreed with me that Jovi was the way to get Mercury to conform to whatever. I told him to give Jovi to me. He thought I was on some pedophile type shit. I had to convince him that I wasn't and that my mother would take good care of her. It took two weeks for me to convince him to let me get Jovi. When he handed her over to me, it was over. I got her and my mother out of town and away from the bullshit. If Kosine tried to go back looking for her, he'd never be able to find them.

***Beep... Beep.... Beeeepppppppp....***

The sound of someone blowing their horn at me startled me. I glanced up and saw that it was Day-Day and them. I shrugged my shoulders at him to see what was up. He motioned for me to pull over, so I did. I figured maybe there was a change of plans or something.

"Yo?" I said, getting out the car and jogging up to his car.

"Yo? Fuck you mean yo? Lyn said something looks wrong with Mercury," Day-Day stated to me.

"The bitch is sleep. What's supposed to be wrong with her?"

"Didn't you pull your gun on her?" Lyn quizzed.

"Yeah. That was because the bitch was hitting me," I told them.

"Hitting you for what?" Lyn asked.

"Wait a minute... You could see me pulling my gun but you ain't see my car swerving when I was trying to get the bitch off me?" I quizzed, scratching my head.

"We didn't know why you were swerving."

"That's when you should've been pulling the car over. The fuck! Y'all weird as fuck. Anyway, there's been a change of plans," I went ahead and told them. I didn't have time to get to New Orleans and end up falling out with them. In order for me to carry out my plan of getting rid of Kosine, I needed them to continue to rock with me. Telling them about Mercury or my real motive was not needed at this time.

"Tell Mercury to come here," Lyn instructed me.

"You can go wake her up and when you do, she's riding with y'all. We ain't been riding long and she's already talking too damn much." I knew they didn't want her to get in the car with them, so I wasn't really worried about her actually getting out of the car to go check on her.

"Fine. I sure will. I don't have a problem with her riding with us. You have a target on your back. She'll be safer with us anyway," Lyn voiced.

"I have a target on my back? You don't think you have one on yours? Ma, you're delusional. Logic is coming for you. In his mind, you belong to him. The fact that you're giving Day-Day his pussy is signing your death certificate," I concluded.

"You don't know shit," she spat and climbed out of the car. That's when I did something I didn't want to do. It had always been my backup plan. They couldn't learn that Mercury was dead or everything that I had done would've been in vain.

Reaching inside my pocket, I found the small button that was in there. Lyn was about to walk toward the car, but I pushed the button. As soon as I did, smoke began coming from my car.

"What the fuck!" Lyn yelled. Day-Day and Yo-Yo looked back to see what she was gasping at. Suddenly, the car went up in flames. It wasn't a bomb or anything, but I had the car rigged to spark a fire and that's exactly what it did. It started under the hood and spread quickly. Lyn fell down to her knees in tears, yelling Mercury's name.

"We gotta go," Day-Day hollered.

"We can't leave her. She has a daughter," Lyn cried.

"She had a daughter. She's fried," I joked. Nobody laughed but Yo-Yo and me.

"That shit not funny. Stop being so muthafuckin' cold hearted," Day-Day fumed. He picked Lyn up and carried her back to the car. Sitting her inside the backseat, he told me to get in the car. We had to leave before the police came.

With everyone inside the car, Day-Day put it in drive and peeled away from the scene. It was sad that Mercury had to go out the way that she did, but I had no other choice. I would've loved for her body to be in one piece so that Jovi would've gotten the chance to see her one last time but that couldn't happen. It was really nobody's fault but her own.

"Aye, you said there was a change of plans. What are the new plans and why the fuck you ain't stop to tell us?" Day-Day asked over all the loud as whooping and hollering Lyn was doing for Mercury. For her to not be fuckin' with her the hard way, she was shole clowning for her like they were the best of friends.

"Kosine called me and said that he wanted to meet at Mercury's mother's house. I'm not sure why. All I can do is go there."

"How the hell are we supposed to get Logic there?"

"Don't worry. He's goin' to get Logic there because he wants me to kill him. Everything is coming together." It sounded better than I thought it was. While he thought I was trying to convince him, I was really trying to convince myself that everything was going to work out. They needed to. I was sick of dealing with all of their asses.

"Aight. Bet. This better not be no bullshit either," Day-Day warned me.

"Yeah. If it is, know that you're a dead man walking," Yo-Yo chimed in. Instead of choosing to respond, I dropped my head. I went back to acting like the same timid as Chico that they expected me to act like. They were feeding right into my hands.

Day-Day continued to drive, and I noticed Yo-Yo dozing off. It was definitely going to be a long as ride but an even longer night. I needed to get my rest as well. Laying my head back on the seat, I shut my eyes and tried to get as much rest as I could in between all of the damn screaming Lyn was doing.

"Get up, nigga." I was awakened by Yo-Yo shaking me. I had to blink my eyes a few times to clear my vision. When it was clear, that was when I realized we were in the neighborhood that Mercury's mother lived in. Lyn must've cried herself to sleep because she was laid back on the seat with her mouth open and tongue hanging out. She looked like she was famished from eating a big meal or something. I laughed on the inside at how crazy her ass was over there looking. I couldn't lie though. Even with the way she was positioned, Lyn was still fine as fuck. There was no question why all of these men were drooling over her the way that they were.

"You ready?" Yo-Yo asked me.

"What's the plan?" I inquired. I needed to know how they planned to help me stay alive, so I'd feel a lot better. It wasn't nobody there but the four of us and Lyn technically was no help. There wasn't shit she could do to help any of us when it came to Logic. She wasn't in this street shit.

"Both of them are there," Day-Day acknowledged, pointing to the cars that were sitting outside the house three doors down. There were several cars so that meant that it was more than the two of them.

"Why the fuck they need so much help for one person?" I quizzed. For the first time, I was regretting my role in all of this shit. I should've accepted my brother's death and moved the fuck on.

"Don't get scared now," Yo-Yo teased.

"Scared now? His ass been scared since he got in this shit." Day-Day laughed. The shit wasn't funny. Yo-Yo stared at me. It was like she was looking through to my soul. For some reason, I felt like she'd figured me out and knew that I wasn't as weak as I was pretending to be.

"Kosine not expecting you to go in there blurting everything out. I'm sure they not expecting for you to get here so soon either. Go in there and surprise their asses. Lay everything out on the table. The tables will turn. Watch. You'll be fine," Day-Day tried to assure me. "Besides, we will be right here if anything pops off," he added. For some reason, I didn't believe his ass.

Slowly, I slid out the backseat of the car and took the

dreaded walk to Mercury's mother's front door. My phone was on so that Day-Day and Yo-Yo could hear everything as it played out. I lifted my hand preparing to open the door, but it swung open before my hand touched the knob.

"Took you long enough, nigga," Kosine stated as he yanked me inside the house. He took me inside the living room where there was a chair sitting in the middle of the floor. Nobody was there but he and I. That worried me. We did all this so that Logic would be here and hear everything that I had to say about Kosine being the one behind trying to kill him.

"What's that chair for?" I asked him.

"For you to sit your punk ass down. You wanted to talk so I'm giving you the floor," he snidely commented. I knew he was on some shit. He was being sarcastic as fuck and the expression on his face was not one that I trusted.

"I'm not about to play with you, Kosine. I don't need to sit in this chair to tell you what the fuck I got to say to you."

"What is it that you have to say?"

"You killed my fuckin' brother. He didn't deserve that shit. You think you can kill people and get away with it?"

"Hell yeah. I've been doing it and ain't shit happened to me yet."

"That's because Logic don't know that you're the one that has been trying to kill him," I blurted out.

"Shut your fuckin' mouth, nigga. You don't know what the hell you're talking about," he stated through clenched teeth.

"Why would I not know what I'm talking about when I was the person that you paid to kill him? You took them innocent people from me thinking you were hurting me, and I didn't give a damn about them. The whole damn time you wanted Logic out of the way and the entire time, I was gunning for you. Why the fuck you think Logic's still alive? That nigga wasn't expecting me, so I could've been killed him. I was always aiming to kill your mufuckin' ass but God must've really been on your side because you always managed to get the fuck out of dodge before the bullet hit your ass," I honestly told him.

"What the hell is he talking about?" Logic came from around the corner and asked.

"I don't know what this punk ass nigga talking about but he not about to be talking much longer," Kosine stated. He raised his gun and aimed it at my head. Logic put his hand up to stop him.

"Naw. Let him talk. I want to hear what he has to say," Logic commented.

"Kosine has been the person gunning for you all this time. He tried to make it seem like Day-Day and Yo-Yo because he was mad that Day-Day refused to work for him. He felt that Day-Day needed to move up and be his right-hand man with you out of the way and he could take over. Things didn't work out in his favor. He was angry that Day-Day not only told him no, but Day-Day was able to get the one person that he couldn't... Lyn." Telling him the truth was the best option for me. It wasn't like I had shit else to lose.

"So, he paid you to kill me, but you didn't? Why?"

"He killed my brother."

"Who was your brother?"

"Rae. RAE WAS MY BROTHER!!! This nigga got mad when he learned that Rae had been fuckin' around with Mercury. Jovi is Rae's child and the new child that Mercury was pregnant with belonged to Rae as well. He couldn't handle everything not working out in his favor, so he killed him. You were the last piece of the puzzle for him to take over. With you out of the way, everything would belong to him." Just call me Tekashi because I had no problem being a snitch at this point. It was either Kosine' s life or mine. At the end of the day, I valued mine way too much to let this slime ass nigga keep getting away with doing innocent people wrong.

"I know you not going to listen to that nigga over me," Kosine shouted.

"Not at all," Logic stated. He raised his gun in the air.

Logic aimed his gun at me. I was furious. After all of the information I'd just presented him with, he still felt compelled to take my life. Truth be told, he owed me his life. If it wasn't for me purposely missing when I was supposed to kill his ass, he would be dead by now. That showed how dirty niggas in these streets were.

Keeping my eyes opened, I locked them in on Logic's eyes. If I was going to die, I was going to die the man I was raised to be. I stood steadfast and awaited my fate. It wasn't long after before those dreaded sounds were heard.

***Pow... Pow... Pow...***

That's when I finally closed my eyes and dropped down to my knees.

## 21

# LOGIC

Lyn calling me should've caused me to be happy. It didn't and something was off. She had to have linked back up with Day-Day's ass. If she didn't learn that I would kill her behind that shit, then she needed to rethink her entire life. I'd already had plans to head back to New Orleans when Kosine called me. So, it was no big deal for me to link up with him. However, when he revealed to me the reason he wanted to go, I knew that he was up to something. Whether he knew it or not, I had been having niggas follow him and I'd been listening in on a lot of his calls. He thought he was walking away to have privacy, but I was like a thief lurking in the night. I'd since learned that he couldn't be trusted.

"Damn, man. You ain't have to kill me. I ain't do shit to you. I ain't even come after you like I was paid to do." Chico was on his knees crying like a bitch. I stood there shaking my head at how pitiful he looked.

"Get yo' dumb ass up," I aggressively spoke after allowing him to wallow in his tears for about ten minutes. He was crying and asking why I had to kill him. That nigga must've been hitting the same shit that Kosine was on for him to not realize that he wasn't dead.

A few more minutes passed before I watched Chico run his hands down his body. He patted himself all over. I'm assuming he was checking for bullet holes.

"Get the fuck up," I punched the wall and demanded. I was upset that I was having to stare at Kosine's lifeless body. He had to have known it was comin'. While he was plotting against me, I was busy plotting against his ass too.

"Yeah... Yeah mufucka'," Chico stood over Kosine and taunted him. "That's what the fuck I thought," he yelled before kicking Kosine a few times.

"Nigga, you slow." I couldn't help but laugh. Kosine must've really had him shook for him to be so hostile to his dead body.

"I thought you were going to kill me. How much of the conversation did you hear?"

"I heard more than enough. Plus, I'd known for a while that he was up to no good. I tried to give him the benefit of the doubt and hoped he would change. It didn't happen. That let me know that I'd always have to look over my back when it came to him and that was not something I wanted to do," I admitted to him. It felt weird to finally say the words I'd been thinking for a long time.

"How long have you known that it was him?" Lyn's voice softly spoke to me, startling me. I closed my eyes thinking I was tripping until I felt someone touch my shoulder. "I'm here," she said to me. I opened my eyes and turned to face her.

"What are you doing here?" I asked, overly excited to see her. I was grinning big as hell until I saw Day-Day and Yo-Yo come walking out from behind her.

"I should've known. So, you came in here to kill me?" I placed my hands around her neck and proceeded to choke her. I was shaking her like a ragdoll. I didn't want to kill her, but she'd betrayed me and at that moment, I was viewing her in the same manner as I'd viewed Kosine. She was a threat to me. Why else would she be there with the enemy? She was my wife. For us, it was until death do us part. If I killed her, I knew they would kill me. That meant that Lyn and I would still be together. In death. That worked for me. That also meant that Day-Day wouldn't have her either.

"Let her go," Day-Day ordered. He pulled out his gun and aimed it at me. Yo-Yo did the same. Slowly, I removed my hands from around Lyn's neck and moved away from her. I kept my hands in the air to let them know that I wasn't a threat. I had to rearrange my thoughts. Killing Lyn might not have been as worth it as I thought in the beginning. I'd end up losing too much. I wasn't ready to give up my power just yet.

"If you want her that bad, you can have her. She's not worth it anyway," I seethed and pushed her away from me.

***Smack...***

Lyn came over to me and smacked me upside the head.

"Fuck you, Logic. I was your mufuckin' prize. I may not have been as small as those other bitches that threw themselves at you but I'm a whole black, educated woman over here. I got my shit together. I've never used you. Everything that we shared was genuine. At least on my end, it was. You didn't deserve me then and you sure the fuck don't deserve me now. You telling someone they can have me is supposed to do what? He already got me. He has me more than your lame ass ever had."

"So, you mad?" I chuckled. She'd grown a big set of balls since fuckin' with Day-Day. She knew never to step to me like that. She would have never done that in the past. That's how I knew this was all his doing.

"I'm not mad. I'm angry as hell. But you know what, I'm going to get Day-Day and Yo-Yo to let you live. You now see that they weren't the ones coming after you despite the shit that you did to them."

The longer I stood there listening to her yapping, the more worried I became. She was mad at me, but I knew she was not the type of person to take a life. She loved me too much for that. She could act like she hated me all she wanted, but I knew her through and through and she wasn't built to be malicious to anyone.

"They know the game. It came to me that they were coming after me. I did what anybody else in my shoes would do. You have to eliminate them before they get you," I called myself explaining to her.

"No nigga. A real boss ass nigga would've checked the facts and learned what was true. Just because Kosine told you what he wanted you to know doesn't mean it was legit. You got mad at Lyn for them sleeping together. Did your boy tell you that he drugged her?" Yo-Yo asked me.

"What?" My palms started itching. My body started warming up. Surely, I didn't hear her correctly. There was no way Kosine did what they said he did. I'd learned everything else about him. Why didn't I know that bit of information?

"They aren't lying. I'm not a cheater. I've never cheated on you and you know that. You can tell me everything else about me, but you never thought about that?"

"I'm sorry." I had no choice but to apologize to her. She was right. I should've known her better. I should've realized that with all of the shit that was going on, Lyn would never betray me like that. Even when it came to Day-Day, she wasn't wrong in choosing to be with him. She thought I was dead, and it wasn't until she learned of my indiscretions with Kazya that she decided to be with him. That's what the average person would've done. Hell, truth be told, if the shoe was on the other foot and she was supposedly dead, I'd have another bitch in my bed by the time nightfall came.

"Let it go because you and I both know you don't mean that. Thanks for that fake act of kindness. At this point, all I want is for you to walk away from me and don't look back. Don't come after me or my man," Lyn told me. She had Day-Day's back the way she used to have mine and I didn't know how to feel about that.

"You know I can't do that. I can't walk away from the love of my life."

"The love of your life. Pfft... Boy, you are out of your mind. You and I both know that I'm only the love of your life when it's convenient for you. Walk away, Logic. Take this as your opportunity for a second chance."

"You better listen to her. You got less than thirty seconds to decide what you're going to do before I start shooting."

"Tell me you want to go with me, and we can leave together. Don't let him scare you into thinking you have to stay with him," I pleaded with her. I didn't want to lose her. It was sad that our relationship had come to this.

"Goodbye Logic. Don't come near me again," she said and turned to leave. I was about to go after her, but Chico and Yo-Yo stood before me. That allowed Lyn and Day-Day time to get out of my sight. I laughed at how Day-Day had his sister come save the day for him. What kind of man was he to have to depend on a bitch to have his back?

"Let her know this shit ain't over," I said to Yo-Yo.

"Oh, but it is. She may have allowed you to live but I promise you that your time is coming. If you come near her again for anything, I swear you'll regret the day you ever met her," Yo-Yo threatened me. Chico never said a word. I was about to respond but opted not to. Lyn had made up in her mind that Day-Day was who she wanted. I knew that was a lie but all I could do was deal with it. She'd be back. Whether she wanted to do it willingly or not. She would be back. I turned to walk away but Yo-Yo stopped me.

"Not so fast," she said.

"What now?" I asked, irritated that she was still in my presence.

"Remember when you put your mufuckin' hands on me? I told you I was going to whoop your ass, didn't I?" she confidently spoke.

Laughing at her was the only thing I could think to do. If she thought she was about to beat my ass, she had the game fucked up. So, I thought. Yo-Yo came charging at me like a bull. The first blow she sent to my head caused my shit to instantly turn to the side. My mufuckin' neck popped at the same time. I got ready to hit her back but couldn't. I was bombarded with blows coming from both her and Chico. I was no match for them. The only thing I could do was protect my face as best as possibly while they beat my ass.

# 22
## LYN

*FOUR MONTHS LATER*

*"I missed you so much. I'm sorry I had to leave you the way that I did," he whispered in my ear doing his best to make up for lost time.*

*"I missed you too. I was so lost without you. You weren't gone long but it seemed like forever," I replied to him before placing my hands around his neck and pulling him in for a passionate kiss. No matter what happened between us, nothing would ever change the way I felt about him. I loved him. He had my heart. That was not something that would just fade away.*

*My baby laid on top of me and was slow grinding inside of me. My head pushed further into the pillow as I gripped his hips and held on. He was pushing deep inside of me. Deeper than he'd ever been. I wasn't complaining at all, but damn. He needed to pull back some. That nigga was so deep inside of me, it felt like he was going to rearrange my damn organs.*

*"Pull back some," I finally told him.*

*"For what? This my pussy. I can go as deep as I want," he quipped.*

*"No, the fuck you can't," I sassed. He had me fucked up. Yeah, I was his woman, but this was still my body. His ass was going to have to*

*respect me. The fact that I had to keep preaching to him about respect was a problem.*

*"Damn. Well at least suck a nigga dick. I missed that shit," he called himself speaking seductively.*

*"Naw. I'm good. You were gone for a lil' minute. I don't know where your dick been," I fussed.*

*"Gotdamn. I can't get shit out yo' ass. You don't want me going too deep or nothing. Damn, the least you could do is suck a nigga dick. That way you can deep throat my shit," he fumed.*

*"I could but I ain't. Gone get your nut so you can get the fuck off me." I was sick of his shit. The more I thought about him being inside of me, the more disgusted I was. How the hell could I even think this would be okay?*

*That nigga didn't waste no time. He started pumping in and out of me like he was pulling a string to start a damn lawn mower. It wasn't a good three minutes later that he was about to nut. I tried to push him off of me because I didn't want him nutting inside of me. It didn't work. He pressed down further and expelled all of his seeds inside of me. He wouldn't even move so I could jump up and go to the bathroom. I was either going to pee or lay in the shower and allow the water to run inside my pussy.*

There I stood pacing back and forth in front of the bathroom mirror. Afraid to pee on the little stick. I'd been feeling sick for a while. I thought it was my nerves after everything that happened these past few months. Then I started eating more, my breasts were tender, I'd see spotting with no period, and I was running to the bathroom damn near every twenty minutes. It was so bad that I went to my doctor to have her check to see if I had diabetes. Those tests came back okay. They checked me for STDs and everything. All of those tests were good. They wanted to give me a pregnancy test, but I refused. I was too afraid of what the results would be. I couldn't delay it much longer. For a while, I didn't even think I could get pregnant. Not after the abortion I had. However, I recently started having these feelings that I may be pregnant

There were some small SOLO red cups that I kept in the bathroom to pour my mouthwash in to gargle with after brushing my teeth. Not wanting to risk losing any pee, I squatted over the toilet and held the cup between my legs. I decided that peeing in the cup would be my best bet and it would give me enough urine to take the test. I damn near wanted to scream when the hot pee started dripping out and was hitting my damn hand. That was the worst feeling in the world. It was times like these that I wished I had a dick. *Damn!*

When I was done, I wiped between my legs and stood straight up. I took the top off the test and dipped it inside the cup until I saw that the stick was fully covered. I did two additional tests. I grabbed three different kinds so there wouldn't be any confusion on if I was or wasn't pregnant. Setting a timer on my phone for three minutes, I sat it down on the counter next to the tests so it would alert me when it was time to check them.

"Aye bae, I'd been calling your name for a minute. You go-" Corde' burst inside the bathroom as I was about to put the last stick down on the sink. It caused me to jump since I wasn't expecting him to come in and I knocked over the rest of the pee that was still in the cup. I thought he'd left the house since he told me he had some errands to run. I'd been waiting for him to leave so I could take the test. He'd been wanting a baby, but I was too scared to bring one into this world. At least not until I knew for sure that he was done with that assassination shit and nobody was going to come after us.

"Bae, you pregnant?" he asked, snatching the stick out of my hand.

"I don't know yet. I was about to wait on the three minutes to pass to find out." I snatched the test back out of his hand and laid it down on the counter.

"Why didn't you tell me that you were taking a test? Shit, why didn't I know that you even thought you were pregnant?"

"This was a spur of the moment thing. I figured something had to be wrong with me since I'd been sick so much."

"Yeah, but you'd been going to the doctor. If you were pregnant, they would've told you. They've ran a million and one tests on you. I'm sure a pregnancy test would've been the first one they did, right?" That is where he was wrong. I never told him that I wouldn't allow them to give me a pregnancy test. He would be furious to know that. So, I kept the shit to myself. Hell, he didn't have to know all my business.

"Maybe it was too soon to tell," I lied.

"Naw. They do fuckin' blood tests and shit. They would've known. Baby, why are you doing this to yourself? We are going to find out what's wrong with you," he stated, trying to make me feel better.

"Can you help me get this pee up?" I asked, changing the subject.

"Yeah. I'll go get the mop." Corde' left out the bathroom to get the mop. I went under the sink and grabbed the bathroom cleaner. I squirted it all around the toilet and on the floor. I got some paper towel and wiped up as much as I could. Corde' came back a few minutes later with the mop and mop bucket.

"I got it," I told him, reaching for the mop. I was still upset that he barged into the bathroom on me and made me spill the damn piss everywhere.

"Move, ma. We not 'bout to do this," he grunted and pushed me out the way.

"Do what? I'm trying to get this mess up that you made," I refuted.

"Naw. You made the mess. All I did was open the door. It ain't my fault you can't hold your piss, ma. Guess you gonna be shitting on yourself next," he joked. I wanted to be mad at his ass, but I couldn't be. I never could stay mad at him and he knew it.

"I swear you make me sick," I teased and pushed him gently. He picked me up and was getting ready to carry me to the bed until the alarm on my phone went off.

"Wait baby..." I stopped him and had him place me back down on my feet.

"What's wrong? I'm trynna dip off in you before Yo-Yo and Chico show up," he expressed. I laughed because of the expression on his face. He didn't crack a single smile.

Since everything that transpired, Chico came on to work with Yo-Yo. Corde' told her that he was no longer interested in that lifestyle. Especially since we'd been talking about starting a family of our own. I thought it was going to be an issue, but Chico had been holding his own. Yo-Yo would try to spazz out on him and he'd give that shit back to her. It made her so mad one time, she kicked the lid off the toilet and tried to hit him in the head with it. He told her quickly that if she hit him, she'd better make sure she killed him because he was going to knock her tonsils down her throat and out her ass. Ever since that incident, them niggas been fuckin' around. Corde' doesn't know they are a couple yet and we are all trying to keep it that way. He might flip his lid if he knew his sister was out their busting it open for someone he once viewed as an enemy.

"Baby, come on. What the hell you doing standing there staring at the fuckin' floor and shit?" he barked, removing me from my thoughts.

"Wait... I need to check these tests," I informed him and then went over to the counter to pick up the first test to check the results.

"For what? They not gonna say sh-"

"Pregnant," I mumbled, stopping him from finishing his statement.

"What you say lil' baldheaded ass girl?" he questioned me, wanting me to repeat what I said.

"I'M PREGNANT IN THIS BIAAAAATTTCHHHHH!!!" I yelled, jumping up and down. It took him a minute to realize what I said. He snatched the test from my hand. His eyes bucked and got bigger. He picked up the other two tests. They all said the same thing. He wouldn't move or speak.

"Corde'?" I called his name.

"Huh? What?" he belligerently spoke.

"I thought you would be happy." The lack of reaction I got from him upset me. I didn't understand why he wasn't jumping up and down and as excited about the pregnancy as I was.

"What? Are you kidding me? I'm ecstatic baby. This is the best news of my life. There's only one thing left for me to do..." he said.

Corde' left out of the bathroom and returned a short while later. He stepped inside the bathroom and walked right up to me. He picked my hand up and placed one of the biggest rings on my finger that I'd ever seen.

"What does this mean?"

"It means you're mine forever. Fuck you talkin' 'bout?"

"You ain't even propose to me," I fussed.

"For what? You and everybody else know what the fuck it is. Don't you forget that! You not no damn baby momma. You're wifey. Remember that shit," he told me before pulling me in and sloppily kissing me. At that point, I was ready to say fuck Yo-Yo and Chico and take MY HUBBY to bed.

"Come on, lemme get a quickie in," he requested. We both knew that there wasn't shit quick that he did. Not when it came to sex. We were bound to be going at it all night.

***Ding...***

My phone went off alerting me of an incoming text. I went over to my phone to see who was texting me. It was from an unknown number. That prompted me to quickly pick it up and see who it was. Anything from an unknown number was never good. Not when it came to the life we lived.

"Who is it baby?" Corde' quizzed.

"I dunno. Go to the bed, here I come," I instructed him. He shrugged his shoulders and walked away.

***504-296-1234:*** Hey baby girl.

***Me:*** Logic?

***504-296-1234:*** Who else would it be? You know I'd never let you get away from me that easily.

***Me:*** You vowed to leave me alone. Stick to your word or I'm going to have to send Corde' to finish you.

***504-296-1234:*** LOL... Yeah right. I know you're not going to do that.

***Me:*** You wanna bet? Leave me alone. I don't want to have this conversation with you again.

***504-296-1234:*** We will be having another serious conversation in five months.

When he said that, I suddenly felt nauseous. I knew exactly what he meant. It seemed like happiness was not something that I was determined to have. Something was always coming in to take it from me.

***Me:*** Go away!

***504-296-1234:*** Ain't no going away. If you don't want Day-Day to know that you slept with me the night that I kidnapped you, I'd suggest you play nice. I'm not with the dumb shit. Not when you could be carrying my seed.

Mentally, I was not prepared to deal with Logic. Me sleeping with him was not by choice. I had to. He was going to kill me. I was doing any and everything I could to stay alive. When Corde' asked me if he touched me, I should've told him the truth then, but I couldn't. I was scared of how he was going to look at me.

***504-296-1234:*** The fact that you have yet to respond tells me everything I need to know. I may not be with you, but I have eyes everywhere. Nothing that you do will go unknown to me. I guess congratulations is in order. I'm going to leave you alone because I don't want to stress my seed. When my baby is born, I'll be back.

***Me:*** How did you know?

***504-296-1234:*** I didn't know. All I heard was that someone saw you buying the pregnancy test. The fact that you just asked me how I know lets me know that you really are pregnant. I can't wait to see you in five months and meet my seed. I love you baby girl. Never forget that. It's me and you until death do us part.

"Where you at, bae? A nigga harder than a brick," Corde' announced, walking inside the bathroom with his dick in his hand. As bad as I wanted to give myself to him, I couldn't. I had to tell him the truth.

"I need to tell you something," I started talking. He threw his hand up to stop me from speaking.

"I already know what it is, and I don't care. That's my seed and you're my wife. Fuck Logic. Now come get this dick before I put your ass on punishment," he remarked and walked out the bathroom like the mufuckin' 'G' that he was.

For the first time in what seemed like forever since I received the text from Logic, I could breathe again. I guess it was finally time for me to have that happiness I always wanted after all. Blessed was the only word to describe it. And all it took was for me to fall in love, really in love, with a down south hoodlum.

***(To Be Continued...)***

Made in the USA
Coppell, TX
18 October 2021

64256074R00099